Zane Likes Kate.
Joanie Likes Kate.
Does Kate Like Girls?

Joanie opened the box and inside was a pair of beaded earrings. They had silver ear hooks, a couple of small translucent blue beads that were kind of pyramid shaped, and in between them was a neat fish-shaped bead that was the same color blue.

"Oh, wow," Joanie said, taking one out of the box. "Did you make these?"

"I did, yes. Do you like them?" Kate bit her lip.

"I love them!" Joanie put the box back into Kate's hands and then took off the earrings she'd worn that day, trading them for the fish. "How do they look?"

Kate looked back at her, smiling in a way that made Joanie melt inside. "Beautiful."

Joanie smiled back, hoping it didn't show. "Thank you so much."

"You're welcome."

"That's so cool that you make jewelry. How do you keep track of all those tiny beads? I'd lose them all over the place."

"It's not that hard, actually." Kate's blue eyes met Joanie's and Joanie felt her heart skip a beat. "I could show you sometime."

"I... I'd like that."

GLBT YA Books from Prizm

Banshee by Hayden Thorne
Changing Jamie by Dakota Chase
City/Country by Nicky Gray
Heart Sense by KL Richardsson
I Kiss Girls by Gina Harris
Icarus in Flight by Hayden Thorne
Masks by Hayden Thorne
Staged Life by Lija O'Brien
The Water Seekers by Michelle Rode

I KISS GIRLS
GINA HARRIS

ILLUSTRATIONS BY ATTA VAZZY

Prizm Books
a subsidiary of Torquere Press, Inc.

I Kiss Girls

I Kiss Girls
PRIZM
An imprint of Torquere Press, Inc.
PO Box 2545
Round Rock, TX 78680
Copyright 2007 © by Gina Harris
Cover illustration by Atta Vazzy
Published with permission
ISBN: 978-1-60370-354-3, 1-60370-354-3
www.prizmbooks.com
www.torquerepress.com

www.prizmbooks.com

Gina Harris

This book is dedicated to the young women and men of the First & Third program at HiTOPS, in gratitude for their time, their truth and their Pride. www.hitops.org

I KISS GIRLS
GINA HARRIS

ILLUSTRATIONS BY ATTA VAZZY

I Kiss Girls

CHAPTER ONE

Joanie, honey! Hurry! The bus--"

"Got it!" Joanie leaped the last two steps and hit the kitchen floor running. "I'm outta here." She grabbed a banana and a slice of toast off the table as she hurried by it, stopping to kiss her mom on the cheek.

"You're late again, stupid," Liz told her.

"Shut up, weenie." Joanie stuck her tongue out at her little sister and headed for the front door at a jog.

"Coat!"

"On it, Mom!" She hefted her bag higher on her shoulder, stuffed her jacket under her arm and sprinted the half a block to the bus stop where Zane, trusty Zane, was holding up the bus for her. He'd stopped just before getting on board, taking his time while pretending to tie his shoe.

Joanie skidded around him and caught the door in one hand. "Good morning!"

"It is now!"

She got on the bus and tossed her bag into a seat. "You rock, Zane."

Zane fell into the seat across the aisle from Joanie and gave her that cute lopsided grin, the same one that made all the freshman girls sigh over him and draw stupid little hearts around his name in their notebooks. "I try."

There were no hearts around Zane's name in any of Joanie's notebooks.

"I thought I was gonna miss it today for sure."

"No way." Zane shook his head. "I wasn't about to let you miss math today."

Joanie rolled her eyes. "I got, like, maybe five hours of sleep. Watch me fail the test."

"Shut up," Zane complained, crossing his arms over his chest. "What's failing for you, Jo, a B?"

"*You* shut up. I get Bs sometimes."

"But not in math."

"Okay, no. Not in math." Never in math. Sometimes in English or history, but she really liked math. She was just good at it, even she wasn't sure why. "You *know* if I get a B on a math test my dad will seriously ground me."

"Damn." Zane shook his head. "But still. That's pretty harsh."

"Yeah, well. I studied my butt off last night."

"And that's why you were late?"

"I overslept." Her answer was deliberately vague. Well, that part was true, she had stayed up too late and overslept, but she wasn't losing sleep over the math test; she'd stayed up late drawing again. Joanie stuffed the rest of her toast in her mouth so she couldn't say anything more. The drawing thing wasn't the issue; he knew she drew comics in her journal, but she didn't dare tell Zane that she'd ended up drawing pictures of his ex-girlfriend, Samantha. She was *so* cute. And so nice.

And so totally straight.

"You wanna hang out tonight?" Zane asked. "I got a new game for my Xbox." The bus hit a bump and the two of them were bounced off their seats. "Jesus."

Joanie grabbed onto the back of the seat in front of her and shook her head. Of all the things she didn't like about school, the stupid bus was at the top of her list. She couldn't wait until senior year, she'd finally have her license and she could drive to school.

If her dad let her have a car.

"Can't tonight, I've got plans."

"Like, *plans* plans?" Zane wiggled his eyebrows at her.

Joanie gave him a look. "No."

Zane leaned closer, speaking softly. "I'm not going to tell anyone you have a date, Jo."

"I don't have a date." She'd love to be lying, but she wasn't. "Who the heck would I be dating?"

"Bummer." Zane shifted in his seat. "Me neither."

Joanie snorted. "I can't imagine why not. You could have your pick of freshman."

Zane rolled his eyes and snarled at her. "Bite me."

Just yesterday, on their way home from town, she and Zane passed at least three freshman girls who waved and said hello to Zane as they walked by. Funny thing was, Zane wasn't out there doing the kinds of things that would get him noticed. He wasn't a jock. He wasn't an actor, either. He wasn't in choir or the orchestra or the ski club. He didn't participate in really anything at all that would make him popular. Quite the opposite, actually. Chess club, chemistry club, computer club, and not a single sport. He was just a guy, a geek even, and Joanie figured he had no idea how adorable he was. That was one of the many reasons that she liked Zane. That, and they could talk about girls together.

Speaking of girls, Samantha walked right by the bus as they got off.

"Hey, Samantha," Zane said, smiling uncertainly and giving his ex-girlfriend a little wave. Joanie could hear the hopeful tone in his voice, but Samantha completely ignored him and kept on walking. Joanie winced. Ouch.

Zane sighed heavily, his shoulders sagging. "Damn."

Joanie never really understood why Samantha and Zane had broken up. Whatever it was, Zane seemed to feel like it was his fault, and he obviously still liked her or he wouldn't try to say hello every time she walked by. Joanie never asked directly, but she figured Zane was at least partly to blame or Samantha would have said hello back.

"There are other girls, Z," she told him, patting his back.

"I guess." Zane let Joanie pull him into the school with her.

Chapter Two

Math was the third class of the morning and it was followed by lunch. Joanie thought the school lunches were pretty disgusting, and she rarely ate whatever hot food they were serving. She could make her own lunches and bring them, but she always forgot to make them the night before and then was always running late in the morning, too. Usually she got a salad and an apple or something like that and that was about it.

She and Zane sat together, as always, poking at their food and looking around the lunchroom.

"So how did the test go for you?" Joanie asked.

"It wasn't bad, actually. You?"

"Cake." Joanie grinned.

"Natch." Zane sighed a something caught his eye. "Oh, look. Today she's sitting with David Arch."

David Arch was on the football team. He was tall and sturdy and, like most football players, he was popular with girls and had a lot of friends. "Zane, forget Samantha."

"Yeah, yeah."

"Seriously, look." Joanie pointed carefully, so only Zane could see. "Over there. Julie Smith."

"What about her?"

"She's cute, right?"

Zane leaned his chin in his palm, pouting. "Julie's stuck up, Jo."

Hmm. That was true enough. "Okay, how about Susan?"

"Susan *Parker*?"

"Yes. Susan Parker. She's pretty, she gets good grades..." Joanie had drawn pictures of Susan in her journal about a year ago when they were in an art class together. Susan was nice. Quiet and kind of shy, but nice.

"Oh, God. No. You know Adam Kennedy?"

Adam Kennedy had asked Joanie out to a movie once in eighth grade. He'd had a mouth full of braces, just like she had at the time and adorable blue eyes, but she just hadn't been interested and she'd turned him down. He'd looked so disappointed. "Yeah, I know Adam. She dated him?"

"Well, sort of. I heard her dad came to the door with a rifle when Adam tried to pick her up once."

Joanie's eyes went wide. "What?"

"Yeah. Adam took her home half an hour before her curfew and never went out with her again."

Joanie winced. "Geez. That can't be true."

"Oh, no? Do you see her with a boyfriend?"

"Well, no..."

"Uh-huh." Zane shook his head. "Psycho Daddy. No way."

Joanie sighed. "Fine. So not Susan. What about..." Joanie looked around the room. Oh.

"Lauren Harper," they both whispered as Lauren walked across the room.

"Yeah."

"Oh, yeah."

Lauren was a cheerleader. She was on the yearbook committee, sang in the choir, played the flute in the orchestra and was the Junior Class Secretary. There were probably other things on Lauren's list of activities that popular overachievers should do, but Joanie couldn't remember what they were. Lauren was beautiful, with long blonde hair and big blue eyes, and despite being one of those high profile girls that was good at everything and had boys falling all over her, she was pretty friendly, too. That almost never happened.

Zane and Lauren watched her until Zane finally pointed out why Lauren wasn't an option. "Damn."

"Ethan?"

Zane nodded. "Ethan."

And that was that. Lauren was taken; everyone knew it. She had been since they were all in eighth grade. Lauren and Ethan were so inseparable that Zane called them "Laurethan", a name that had stuck and had been adopted by lots of kids at school.

The local version of "Brangelina".

Of course, Joanie and Zane had been inseparable forever, too, but everyone knew they were just friends. No one was calling them "Zajoanie" or "Joazane" or anything.

At least, Joanie hoped to hell not.

"Give it up, Joanie, and face it. We know all of these girls."

"Not all of them," Joanie protested. "There are some we barely ever see."

"Okay, most of them."

He was right; there wasn't much point in arguing with him. "Well if it makes you feel any better, I can't get a date either."

Zane looked at her. "We'll just be single together then. I don't need a girlfriend, right?"

Joanie smiled. "Yeah? Well, me neither."

Zane bumped shoulders with her. "We're good."

After school, Joanie called her mother from her cell phone to tell her she was going to hang out at Zane's. Her after school 'plans' had been to just go home and draw, but it seemed like Zane needed some company so she told him they'd been cancelled.

"Are you staying for dinner?"

"I don't know, Mom. Maybe?"

Her mother sighed. "Yes or no, Joanie, I need to know."

"Yes, then."

"Okay. If you walk home, please call me first so I know you're on your way."

"Yes, Mom."

"And say hello to Zane for me."

Joanie snorted into the phone. "Bye, Mom." Joanie's mom was convinced that she and Zane were boyfriend and girlfriend, no matter how many time Joanie told her they were just good friends. Joanie had given up arguing about it ages ago.

They got off the bus and, instead of parting ways or heading to their hang out spot at the graveyard, Joanie went with Zane to his house. The house was empty; Zane's mom was a nurse and she worked weird hours and his dad worked in the city and usually wasn't home until after seven. Zane didn't have any sisters or brothers either. Joanie sometimes envied how he had the house to himself all the time, but she mostly she just felt bad for him..

"Hungry?"

"I'm not the bottomless pit you are, Z."

"Shut up. I know you want popcorn." Zane waved a bag at her.

Joanie laughed. "You don't have to be hungry to eat popcorn." She leaned on the counter while Zane put the bag in the microwave and got them each a Coke, and picked up a magazine with Avril Lavigne on the cover. "Oh, ho! Someone's got a crush."

Zane looked over his shoulder and shrugged. "What? She's pretty."

"Please." Joanie rolled her eyes. "What's with the eye makeup thing? She looks like she's going to take a big bite out of your neck any minute." She flipped a page. "Ah, Emma Roberts. Now she is pretty."

"Show me?"

Joanie held up the magazine.

"Oh, yeah. Definitely. Wow."

"Oh! And Vanessa Hudgens."

"She's the High School Musical chick?" Zane asked.

"Yep."

"Yeah." Zane nodded. "She has nice eyes. And I love her hair. I'd totally date her."

Joanie sighed. "She'd probably go for you, too." Who wouldn't? Zane was a serious catch – for a straight girl. "At this point I'd date one of your mom's tacky kitchen chairs if it claimed to be a lesbian and asked me out."

"Oh, come on, Jo. It's not that bad."

"What do you know about it, Zane? You could have a date tonight if you wanted one."

"Yeah. With a freshman."

"Hey, it's a date." Joanie tossed the magazine back on the table and crossed her arms over her chest. "When was the last time you kissed a girl?"

"What?"

"Tell me."

"Well, it was Samantha." Joanie didn't need to look at Zane to know he was blushing. "So... maybe a month ago?"

"Uh-huh. Now ask me."

"Jo..."

"Go on, Zane. Ask me."

Zane shook his head at her as he brought over a bowl of popcorn, but he asked. "Fine. When was the last time you--"

"Never."

"Jo..."

"No, really, Zane. Never."

"You've never kissed a girl?"

"Or a guy for that matter. Careful there, your eyes might pop out of your head."

"Geez."

"See? So quit your complaining, I don't want to hear it. I listened to you go on and on and *on* about Samantha for months."

"Shit, I'm sorry."

"Uh-huh. I don't even know what it's like to kiss anyone." Joanie reached into the bowl and grabbed a handful of popcorn, which she shoved into her mouth before grabbing the whole bowl from Zane and heading for the living room. She flopped on the couch and put the bowl in her lap. Zane sat their Cokes down on the coffee table in front of them and sat next to her.

"You wanna kiss me?"

Joanie looked at him. "What? Ew. No."

"What do you mean 'ew'? I'm serious. Then at least you could say you know what it's like."

Joanie glanced at him. "No."

Zane shrugged and reached for the popcorn. There was a long silence between them while they both munched and sipped their Cokes. Joanie finally looked at him again.

"...you're serious?"

Zane laughed. "Yeah, sure. Why not? I'm safe at least. You know. I'm not going to go bragging to anyone or anything." Zane gave Joanie a toothy grin and Joanie shoved him backward.

"No."

"You sure?"

Well, Zane had a good point. He was safe and Joanie trusted him. If she wanted to know, he was as good as anyone to find out with. But there was still one more thing...

"You'll never let me live it down."

Zane tried to look offended. "I won't tease you, I swear."

"You'll make fun of me."

"Seriously, I won't! I promise."

"You promise?" Joanie squinted at him.

"Absolutely. Promise."

"You swear on your Xbox?" While most people went to church or whatever, Zane worshiped at the altar of his video games.

"I swear, Jo. I'll never tease you about it. I'm just trying to be a friend."

"And you're not trying to get a cheap thrill?"

"Jo!"

Joanie shrugged. "Right. Okay, then." She set the bowl of popcorn down on the table and turned on the couch so she was facing Zane.

"No big deal, right? Just a kiss."

"Right." Joanie agreed. "But why couldn't you be a girl?"

Zane grinned at her again. "I could put on some heels…"

Joanie hit him.

"Sorry. Ready?"

Joanie nodded, but as Zane leaned forward, she suddenly turned away and started to laugh.

"Joanie!"

"Sorry! Sorry," she said, still giggling. "This is just too weird, you know?" Zane gave her a look with an arched eyebrow and she quieted down. "Okay, okay. Seriously, I'm sorry."

"Are you ready now, princess?"

Joanie snorted at him. "Yes."

This time Joanie closed her eyes and let Zane kiss her. It was soft at first, gentle, but then he leaned into her a little bit so that she had to reach out and grab his shoulder or else she might fall over backwards. It was a short kiss, and when Zane pulled away she opened her eyes and blinked at him.

"There."

Joanie frowned. "That's it?"

"What do you mean 'that's it'? That was a kiss! And one of my better ones, too."

"Pfft. That was boring as hell." It was, too. Totally dull.

18

"Shut up!" Zane threw a pillow at her.

"What? I'm not into you, Z, what did you expect? Fireworks? An earthquake?" Joanie threw the pillow back and the next thing she knew Zane had pounced on her and was tickling her ribs.

"Oh, my God! Stop, Z!" she gasped. "Zane!" Joanie wiggled and writhed on the couch and tried to get away but Zane's stupid long legs had her pinned. "ZANE!!"

"Tell me I'm the man!" Zane demanded.

"What?" Joanie was still giggling and her hands fought with Zane's but she was getting nowhere. "You're a jerk!"

"Zane's the man!"

"Cut. It. Out!"

"Say it!"

Joanie gave up. She was laughing so hard that could hardly breathe anymore. She gulped in as much air as she could manage between giggles and shouted. "Zane is the man! Now get the hell off of me!"

Zane moved away looking smug and Joanie growled at him.

"That's right."

"No fair tickling me."

"You said my kiss was boring. I'm hurt." Zane pretended to pout, but there was a great big smile behind it.

"I can't believe I let you talk me into that."

"Damn, here I was trying to help you out and this is the thanks I get?"

"Okay. Okay, Zane. You can kick my butt on your Xbox. Will that make you feel better?" Joanie sighed and reached for her coke.

"It might, rabbit. It just might."

CHAPTER THREE

"Joanie! You're going to be…"

"Latelatelate!" chirped Liz.

"Nope!" Joanie grabbed a banana and a Pop Tart and ran for the door. As usual.

"Coat!"

"Way ahead of you, Mom!" Joanie called back cheerfully.

"Have a good day!"

Joanie ran out the door. For once, the bus wasn't at the bus stop yet. Zane waved but Joanie didn't take the time to wave back, she just kept on running because the bus was pulling up to the curb. Shaking her head at herself, she sprinted the last few yards, stopping by the bus' open doors.

"Oh, after you," she said, grinning at Zane and panting.

"Why, thank you," Zane laughed and climbed on ahead of her. "Such chivalry."

Joanie winked. "Hey, I can be a gentleman when I need to be."

Zane slipped into a seat laughing at her and Joanie fell in beside him still trying to catch her breath.

The bus stopped at school and they got off it together, one after the other, heading inside to hit their lockers before finding their seats in homeroom. They'd chosen lockers right next to each other back in September, a privilege they'd earned for being on the honor roll the year before. As long as they kept their grades up, they would keep these lockers forever. They often joked about which one of them would blow their GPA and have to move out of the "nice" neighborhood first.

The inside of Zane's locker door was plastered with pictures. Some of them were pictures of things he'd done and postcards of the cool places he'd been with his family, one or two were of him and Joanie, but most of them were of stupid Avril Lavigne. Joanie had no idea when that obsession had started, but she was already plotting ways to end it.

Joanie's locker was pretty bare except for a postcard Zane had sent her from Niagara Falls, a mirror where she could make sure her hair was okay before going to class, and a picture of her cat, who she had named Mr. Fuzzbutt, but her mother had changed to Smokey.

Joanie still called him Mr. Fuzzbutt anyway.

They unloaded their heavy backpacks, keeping just the books they'd need for the next few classes, then headed for homeroom. When they walked in, there was a girl that Joanie didn't recognize talking with their teacher, Mr. Foster, by the blackboard. She was a little taller than Joanie, with long, wavy brown hair, and she had on a skirt that hung to her calves that just covered the tops of really nice brown, dressy boots.

"Hey, Fos," Zane said, giving Mr. Foster a wave as they walked past his desk. Zane didn't seem to give the new girl a second look, but Joanie was already intrigued by her hair.

"Morning, Zane, Joanie. Oh! Hey, Joanie, come up here a minute, would you?"

"Teacher's pet," Zane teased quietly and poked her with his elbow. Joanie shot him a look and then went back toward Mr. Foster.

"Hi, Mr. Foster. What's up?"

"Joanie, this is Kate Dalton; she's new and is going to be joining our class starting today."

"Hi," Kate said, sounding a little shy, or maybe just a little nervous. She didn't look nervous at all, though. She smiled at Joanie, and Joanie tried to smile back, but ended up just blinking at Kate for a moment.

"Uh. Hi," Joanie finally managed to say, instead of 'wow, your eyes are *so blue*', which was the first thing that had come to her mind. Kate's eyes were a deep, dark blue, and they seemed to sparkle like stars. Kate's cheeks were rosy and she had soft brown freckles on her nose.

"I told Kate that you were someone that might have time to help her get caught up in trigonometry."

"Oh." Math. Of course.

"Only if you want to," Kate said uncertainly. "I mean, if you don't that's cool. I'm sure can find someone else."

"Huh?" Joanie blinked again, trying to catch up. She'd obviously missed part of the conversation.

Kate put a hand on her arm. "Are you okay?" she asked, looking worried. That was when Joanie realized that she was still staring.

"Oh! I... yes. Fine! I'm sorry. Just... tired. Trig, sure,

no problem." Joanie forced a smile and tried to relax. God, how embarrassing. She hoped she wasn't blushing. "Happy to help."

Mr. Foster smiled at her. "Great. I've given Kate the last week's worth of assignments, maybe you can help her catch up this week during X-period."

Joanie nodded. "Sure, yeah."

"Thanks, Joanie," Kate smiled again and Joanie just stood there stupidly. The bell rang making Joanie jump but at least it brought her back to reality. Homeroom. Class. Right.

Mr. Foster headed for his desk. "Try to get more sleep, Joanie, huh?"

Joanie rolled her eyes.

"Thanks a lot," Kate said. "I'll see you at X-period." She hurried to a desk on the far side of the room by the windows, which must have been the seat that Foster had assigned to her.

Joanie turned around and walked to her desk trying to pretend she didn't see the look that Zane was giving her. Zane's assigned seat was right behind Joanie's and he grinned broadly at her as she walked toward him.

"She's cute." Zane poked her as she sat down. "Really cute."

Joanie just nodded back at him. Kate was more than just cute, she was beautiful. She was the most beautiful girl Joanie had ever seen.

Zane kicked her chair making Joanie turn around. "What?"

"So, what did Fos want?"

"Oh, he asked me to help Kate get caught up in trig."

"Kate?"

"The new girl."

"Wow. Really?" Zane looked over toward the windows and Kate.

"Yeah."

"And are you going to do it?"

"Of course. She's... nice." Nice. That was neutral enough that Zane might not tease her.

Zane snorted. "Brown-noser." He brushed off the end of his nose with two fingers.

Joanie glared at him. "Shut up, Zane," she snapped, and then turned around to face the chalkboard.

"Geez, I was only joking."

Joanie ignored him as Mr. Foster started roll call.

CHAPTER FOUR

Zane caught up with Joanie at lunch. "Are you mad?"

"No, I'm not mad." Joanie really couldn't stay mad at Zane for long, he was her best friend. They had always been like brother and sister that way, they'd bicker, stomp around and pout for a while, and then they'd get over it. "I just hate it when you..." Joanie stopped and collected her thoughts. "Just because I get As sometimes doesn't make me a brown-noser or teacher's pet or whatever you think I am."

"Come on, I was joking, Jo."

Joanie put her tray down at one end of an empty table. "I know. But still--"

"Is it okay if I join you guys?"

Joanie looked up at the voice, but Zane beat her to answering. "It's a big table."

Kate looked at him, and then at Joanie. She seemed a little uncertain.

"Don't listen to him, Kate. He's a jerk." Joanie patted

the seat next to her and Kate smiled, moving around to take it.

"Thanks."

"I am not a jerk," Zane protested.

"Okay. He's a nice guy, but he has no manners."

Kate laughed.

Joanie expected a smart remark from Zane in return but when none came she looked over at him. He was staring at Kate, kind of the way Joanie had in homeroom that morning. Joanie felt herself scowl.

"Oh, I forgot water," Kate said, standing up again. "I'll be right back."

They both watched her go and when she was out of earshot Joanie kicked Zane under the table.

"Ow!"

"Close your mouth, Casanova, you're drooling."

"Yeah. She's kind of... wow."

Joanie shook her head. "Beautiful?"

"Yeah. Really pretty."

"Oh, come on!" Joanie threw up her hands in frustration. "Don't go there, Zane."

"Why not?"

"Just... because. Not this time. Okay?"

Zane snorted. "What's the... Oh." Zane leaned in closer. "You have a little crush on Kate, do you?"

Joanie's eyes grew wide and she leaned in also. "I do not!" she whispered loudly.

"*That's* why you said you'd help her with trig, right?"

"What? No!"

"Uh-huh."

"I said I'd help her out – actually I said I'd help *Mr. Foster* out – because Kate's new and... well, she seems nice. And it's gotta suck, changing schools in the middle of the year and everything."

Zane laughed. "Listen to you."

"What?"

"You're making up excuses."

"I am not!"

"So, is the food always this... *gray*?" Kate asked, cutting off their conversation as she sat down.

Joanie straightened up again feeling self-conscious, but Zane jumped right in with an answer. "It sucks. But it's usually a step or two above dog food."

Kate poked at something that Joanie thought was meant to be a breaded chicken patty with her fork.

"I'm Zane, by the way."

Kate smiled. "Nice to meet you."

"If there's anything you need, you just let me know."

"Thank you."

"I mean, because I just want to make sure you feel welcome. It's a big school, you know?" Zane leaned on his elbow, chin in his palm and smiled back at Kate. His style of flirtation was about a subtle as an anvil falling from the sky. If she'd been Wile E. Coyote, it would have squashed her flat by now.

Kate glanced at him and then looked back at her food. "Right. Thanks."

"Ow!"

"So, where did you move from?" Joanie changed the subject after kicking Zane in the shin again.

Zane sulked. "Stop that."

"I'm from Chicago." Kate answered. If she'd noticed their exchange, she didn't let on. "My father got a promotion out here. My mother and I were going to wait until summer to move out but then she got a good offer, too, so we moved now instead."

"I was in Chicago once. In January. It was freezing." Joanie remembered how the icy wind blew across her face, making her cheeks hurt and her eyes water. "Pretty, though, all that snow."

"Yeah, it was cold in the winter and hot in the summer. But I'm still going to miss it, I think."

Joanie nodded, not sure what to say to that. If her parents picked up and moved tomorrow she wasn't sure she'd miss anything at all. Well, she'd miss Zane, she'd miss their little hideout in the graveyard maybe, but she wouldn't miss the school or the town at all. Part of her was secretly envious of Kate's opportunity to start over.

"You'll learn your way around here in no time," Zane said, taking advantage of Joanie's silence.

"I hope so. It's just a lot, you know? New house, new bus, catching up to everyone. I heard there's going to be a chemistry test on Friday so now I'm going to be even farther behind." Kate shrugged. "Just kind of sucks."

Zane bit, snared like a fish on a hook. "Hey, I can totally catch you up in chem, you know."

Kate looked up from her food. "Yeah?"

"Sure! Joanie's the math genius and don't ask me about *Catcher in the Rye* or whatever, but chemistry is my thing, man," Zane said, straightening up a little in his seat. "You want to try the test on Friday, I can help you out."

Joanie glared at him, but he didn't seem to notice.

Kate looked hopeful, and she smiled at Zane in a way that made Joanie's heart speed up. She was so pretty when she smiled, her eyes just shining. Too bad the smile wasn't for her. It was for Zane. As usual.

"Well, if it would keep me from getting even more

behind…"

"We could do like an hour after school every day or something? Just to figure out where you were at your school and get you ready for the test."

"Zane, that would be so great. Are you sure you wouldn't mind?"

"No problem."

"Awesome." Kate looked at Joanie. "I see what you mean. Nice guy."

"He's a peach," Joanie said dryly.

Kate seemed to settle a bit after that; she even seemed more enthusiastic about her lunch. Joanie poked at her salad, staying mostly quiet while Kate and Zane talked, lost in her own thoughts. As hard as she tried not to be, Joanie was still jealous. Kate was seriously the most beautiful girl she'd ever met, but of course Kate would go after Zane – Zane, the handsome one, the smart one, the *guy*. Joanie would have been more pissed off at Zane, but it didn't really matter, it's not like Kate was interested in her anyway. The girls never were.

Joanie thought again about how nice it might be to move. Ellingwood just got smaller by the day.

CHAPTER FIVE

X-period was a forty-five minute open period during the school day. Some kids had choir practice, some went to ski club meetings or student council meetings or whatever. Like Zane, Joanie wasn't really interested in most of the school clubs and so it was often a free period for her, but today she waited outside the library for Kate because she'd promised to help her catch up in math.

Kate showed up five minutes late. With Zane. It was a good thing he didn't stick around because Joanie wasn't sure she'd be able to say anything nice to him just then.

"I'll catch you later," Zane said giving Kate a pat on the shoulder. "See you later, Jo."

"Yeah. See ya'." Joanie watched him go.

"Hey, Joanie." Kate's voice got a little softer. Joanie looked at her for a minute, wondering, but decided it was probably because they were outside the school library.

"Zane says you two are best friends?"

Joanie looked at Kate. "Yeah, I guess so." Didn't feel

much like it at that moment though.

"He's nice. Cute."

"That's what all the girls tell me, yeah." She changed the subject. "You wanna get started?" Joanie stepped aside and held open the library door for Kate.

About half an hour later, there was good news and bad news. The good news was that Kate wasn't really behind in math at all. She was confused about a couple of things and she had some homework to catch up on, but otherwise she was pretty much up to speed with everyone else. There wasn't supposed to be a quiz until after the weekend, so Kate had lots of time to do the practice exercises, too.

But that was also the bad news as far as Joanie was concerned. Kate didn't need much help it seemed, so Joanie figured there weren't going to be many more X-period tutoring sessions. She had the feeling, because things always worked out that way for her, that Kate wasn't going to be as cool in chemistry. Joanie did her best to shake off the bitter taste that left in her mouth. Not Zane's fault, she kept telling herself.

But man, sometimes she got tired of him being the golden child.

They'd come to a natural stopping point so they decided to quit tutoring for the day and let Kate do some work at home.

"X-period is in the morning tomorrow. If you want, we could get together to go over the homework before class." Joanie suggested.

"That would be great, Joanie. You guys are being so cool. I was really dreading walking into a new school, I'm really glad I met you both."

"Well, you know, I'm just brown-nosing," Joanie said,

leaning back in her chair. Her tone was more sarcastic than she'd intended it to be.

Kate looked at her and then started to laugh. The sound was light and not forced at all, just really genuine. Joanie hadn't really meant it as a joke, but she caught the bug and she couldn't help but giggle with Kate.

"Shh!" A kid at the next table glared at them.

They both got quiet for a second or two and then broke out in even more laughter. Joanie stood up and gathered up her stuff as quickly as possible and she and Kate hurried out of the library.

"Oops!" Kate said as the library door closed behind them.

"You're trying to get me in trouble, huh?" Joanie said accusingly. "New girl. I see how it is."

"What? It was your joke."

Joanie gave Kate a sly look. "How do you know I was joking?"

"Oh, please. You hardly look like the brown-noser type."

Joanie smiled. "Thank you. Tell Zane that if you get a chance, would you?"

Kate snorted.

"Yeah, never mind, he won't believe you anyway."

The period bell rang. "What's up next for you?"

"English. B Wing, um..." Kate pulled her schedule out of her pocket. Joanie was used to seeing everyone with schedules in their hands for the first couple of weeks of school, but usually by this time everyone knew where they were going. Kate was really going to stand out as new. "Room 3B."

"Cool. I've got history in B Wing, I'm headed that way. Come on."

***

Needless to say, Zane wasn't on the bus home. Joanie sat in her usual seat and looked out the window, feeling sorry for herself. If Kate and Zane were getting along, good for them, right? Zane had complained that the girls in their class didn't interest him much, so really Joanie knew she should be happy for him.

But it was hard to ignore that nagging little voice in her head. It kept telling her things like if Zane and Kate got together, he wouldn't need Joanie as much. Kind of like what happened with Samantha. Hell, if Joanie had a girlfriend, she wouldn't be spending as much time with Zane either, that was just how it was. But Zane would get another girlfriend eventually, whether it was Kate or someone else. Joanie might very well be alone right up to graduation.

Usually, Joanie and Zane would hang out for an hour or so in the graveyard before going home for supper, but today, since he was *busy*, Joanie went straight home. Liz was sitting at the kitchen table doing homework.

"You're early!" Liz called out as she came through the door. "Uh oh. You don't look happy. Did Zane get detention again?"

"Haha." Joanie dropped her stuff on a chair and headed straight for the refrigerator. "No." The only time Zane had ever been in detention, Joanie had been right there with him. She didn't really want to repeat that experience. Man, had her dad been pissed off.

"Mom says don't eat the stuff in the blue Tupperware thing."

"What is it?" Joanie squinted at it.

"Something for that diet she's on."

Joanie's mom was Queen of the Fad Diet. Scarsdale, Atkins, Slim Fast, South Beach, the Hollywood Diet, Nutrisystem – you name it, she'd tried it. Joanie thought they were all stupid.

"Ew." Joanie reached past the Tupperware and pulled a can of Coke. She looked down at Liz's paper as she headed for the junk food cabinet. "What are you working on?"

Liz sighed dramatically. "Oh, I have a stupid project due tomorrow."

"Yeah? On what?"

"I'm supposed to look through magazines and cut out five things that remind me of each of my family members."

"Yeah? Sounds like fun. Want help?" Joanie stuck some popcorn in the microwave and sank into a chair next to her little sister.

"I'm having trouble thinking up five things."

"Well, okay. Who are you working on now?"

"Daddy." Liz slid her paper over so Joanie could see it better.

"Right. Dad. Well, okay. Dad plays golf a lot..."

Liz pointed to her paper. "Yep. Got that one."

"And he works in the city."

"Oh, yeah! That's a good one." Liz took notes, writing down the word "city".

"He's... um..." Joanie scratched her head. The microwave beeped and she got up. "He drives that ugly Lexus."

"Uh oh. Don't let him hear you say that."

Liz and Joanie both looked up. "Mom!" they said in unison.

"Don't worry, I think it's ugly, too." Joanie's mom

winked. "I hate the color."

Everyone laughed.

"I was kind of thinking... oh! He's a Yankee fan!"

"Yes!" Joanie gave Liz a high five. "Good one, squirt."

"What are you working on?" their mom asked, leaning over Liz's shoulder.

"It's a project for school."

Joanie's mom nodded. "Don't eat too much, Joanie, I made macaroni and cheese for supper."

"Yes!" Joanie would put aside everything for her mom's mac and cheese.

"See you two later." Her mom headed back out of the kitchen and they heard the stereo turn on in the study. She liked to listen to classical music and knit to relax.

Joanie had not only inherited her mom's hair and brown eyes, but she'd also inherited her mother's creativity and need for quiet alone time. They didn't talk much, mostly because they seemed to argue all the time. Whenever Joanie and her mom got upset with one another, her dad would always telling Joanie that it was because she and her mom were so much alike. Joanie saw the physical resemblance, but the rest kind of confused her. She'd always wanted to be more like her dad, more easy going and friendly.

She looked back at Liz's paper. "Okay, so you need, what? Two more?"

"One. I just got jogging shoes."

"Yeah, okay. And... what else? Oh! Pie."

"Yes! Pie!"

"Apple pie." Joanie nodded. Her dad could eat pie every night. He could eat pie for breakfast. He didn't want birthday cakes; he wanted birthday pie.

"Who next?"

"Well, I already did Mom, she was easy."

"Yeah?"

"Yeah." Liz looked down at her list. "Knitting, cats, music, cooking and hugs."

Joanie smiled. The list was perfect, especially the part about hugs. Her mom had a different kind of hug for every occasion. "How are you going to find hugs in a magazine?"

Liz frowned. "I don't know, but it's the most important thing so I will just have to look hard."

"I'll help." Joanie took her history book out of her bag and sat down at the table with her popcorn. "Who's next?"

"You."

"Oh, well I can't help you with me. Maybe we should do Grandma next."

"It's only people that live in my house, dummy," Liz said with a roll of her eyes.

"You're the dummy."

"You are."

"Want some popcorn, dummy?" Joanie offered the bowl.

"Yes, please. Oh! That's a good one for you."

"What?"

"Popcorn."

Joanie laughed. She did eat a lot of the stuff. At least a bag a day.

"And Justin Timberlake," Liz teased.

"Yeah, right. With a big red circle and a line through it."

"David Bowie, then."

"Better."

"And cats, like mom." Liz was writing furiously.

"Sure."

"And... math. You're good at math."

"I like math, yes."

"And the last one is easy."

"Yeah?"

"Yeah. Best friends."

Joanie looked at Liz. "I'm your best friend?"

"Duh! You're my big sister," Liz said in that condescending sister tone of hers. "*Of course* you're my best friend."

Joanie's bad day suddenly got a hundred times better. Grinning broadly, she threw her arms around Liz's shoulders and kissed her on the cheek. "Thank you, brat."

"Ew!" Liz pushed at her. "You didn't have to do *that*."

Joanie laughed and opened up her text book. *Yeah I did*, she thought, but she didn't say it out loud.

They had hamburgers and macaroni and cheese for dinner. Joanie only ate half the burger but she stuffed herself on the rest.

"How'd the math test go today?" Joanie had been expecting the question.

"Fine," she answered.

"Fine, as in good?"

Joanie nodded. "Really good, Dad."

Her father nodded. "Good, good." He took a sip of his water.

"See?" Liz chimed in. "You *are* good at math."

Joanie smiled at her and winked.

"So, Joanie," her dad asked, chewing on a bite of salad. "The junior prom is only a couple of months away, right?"

Oh, God. Joanie didn't want to talk about the prom, especially not with her dad.

"Yeah, so?"

"And…" He glanced at Joanie's mom who nodded at him and then went back to eating like she hadn't been the one to push Joanie's dad into asking. "Do you have a date yet?"

"Nope."

"Just wondering," her dad said, trying to drop the subject. Sadly, Mom wasn't going to let it go. She sighed at Joanie's father, and then took up the questioning herself.

"Surely there must be someone you'd like to go with, though?"

"You guys." Joanie rolled her eyes. "Knock it off, will you? I don't even think I want to go."

Her mom put her fork down. "Of course you do, sweetheart."

"Claire." Her dad shot a look at her mother, who sighed and sipped her water. "No one is saying you have to go, Joanie, but you should think about it. Are you sure you want to miss your junior prom?"

She didn't want to miss it, actually; she just didn't want to go with some random guy she wasn't interested in. She wanted to go with someone who meant something. Someone she could dance with and hold hands with. A girlfriend. Not that her parents knew that.

Joanie just shrugged at her dad.

"Has Zane asked you?"

Joanie snorted. "Zane and I are just friends, Dad, I keep telling you that."

"He doesn't have a girlfriend right now, does he? Since he broke up with Samantha..."

Joanie leaned back in her chair and crossed her arms. "I'm not going with Zane, Mom, okay?"

"Well maybe Zane has a friend," her mom suggested.

"No."

"You could ask."

"No!"

"But sweetheart--"

"No! Just no, okay? No! Stop asking, and stop... pushing. Just... stop it! Okay? God!" Joanie pushed away from the table and got up, tossed her napkin in her plate and ran up the stairs, slamming the door to her room.

She let herself cry for a while, not even really knowing why. It was just... everything. School, Zane, Kate, the prom, her parents – she was just mad at everybody. And what made her even madder was that she couldn't just be angry without crying. Stupid tears. Stupid prom.

Stupid Zane and his adorable smile.

Stupid pretty straight girls.

She'd finally calmed down when the phone rang. She reached for the receiver to pick it up. "Hello Zane," she said, without needing to look at the caller ID.

"Dude, Kate is so awesome."

"Ugh!" Joanie hung up on him. Of course it rang again a second later, as she knew it would.

"What?" she snapped into the phone.

"Hey, are you pissed at me?"

"Yes, shithead, I'm pissed at you."

"About Kate?"

"I like how you stepped right up there, Mr. Chemistry Tutor."

"Joanie..."

"I offer Kate some math help and I'm a brown-noser. But you? You flirt a little with her and offer some help in chemistry like it's the goddamn Holy Grail and you're a *gentleman*. Way to go.

"Whoa, Joanie."

"So, have you kissed her yet? Did you make out over your text books?"

"Jo, don't be like that. Come on."

"You suck, Zane." Joanie sighed. She hung up the phone again.

It was a minute or two before the phone rang again. This time Joanie picked it up without saying anything, she just sighed into the phone.

"You're really mad at me," Zane said softly.

There was a long silence before Joanie spoke. "I'm upset, Zane," she said truthfully. "But I'm not really mad at you, I guess, I'm just... really frustrated. With everyone. And really sick of living in a town full of straight girls. And really... Ugh! I'm sorry."

"Are you okay?"

"No. I'm not okay. My stupid parents are asking about the prom already."

"Oh," Zane was quiet for a minute. "Joanie, I said I'd take you..." he said softly. But they'd already had this conversation and Zane knew how she felt about that.

Joanie fell back on her bed and put an arm over her eyes. "I know, Zane, but I seriously don't want to go with you. I mean, I don't mean that in a bad way. You're a sweetheart to offer, you know that? And I know you mean well, I just... I want to have a *real* date."

"Hang on, I'm gonna close my door." She heard Zane's door shut and then the squeak of his desk chair. She hated that ugly, squeaky thing and had tried to get him to ask for a new one for Christmas this year but all he wanted was more games. "So are you going to... I mean, maybe you need to tell them, you know?"

"God, that is so going to suck."

"How do you know? Maybe it won't."

"Oh, trust me, it will. I mean, it's not like they'll disown me or anything, it's just... I know they're going to be disappointed."

"Right. Disappointed. And Joanie Pierce never disappoints anyone."

"Shut up." Joanie covered her eyes with one hand. "God, you can be such an asshole."

"Joanie, think about it. You always go out of your way not to let them down. Grades, and everything else. Why do you do that?"

"Because they love me?"

"That makes no sense."

Joanie sighed and slipped onto the floor to lean against the foot of her bed. "I hate this."

"You want me to come over?"

"No, no. Not tonight, I just need to think for a while, okay? But I'll see you on the bus tomorrow."

"Yeah. Try to be on time, will you? I'm sick of looking like the geek that can't tie his own shoes."

Joanie laughed. "I'll be early tomorrow. Okay?" There was a knock on her door. Joanie sighed. "I gotta go."

"Okay. See you tomorrow."

Joanie hung up the phone and took a deep breath. She'd been thinking about telling her parents for a long time now, she just hadn't gotten up the courage yet. She had no idea how. And in any case, she definitely wasn't telling anybody anything tonight.

But someone was knocking so she was going to have to

tell them something. She took a deep breath and opened the door but no one was there.

Just a piece of apple pie with ice cream melting over the top.

Chapter Six

It was raining the next morning, and really cold, too. Just her luck that of all days to have promised Zane she'd be early, Joanie had to pick this one. She tucked her scarf tighter around her neck and hid from the rain under a clear plastic umbrella, wishing she'd remembered her ear muffs. She wasn't a fan of hats; they tended to flatten out her artfully spiky hair, but a girl had to keep her ears warm, right? She could have used some mittens, too.

"Hey." Zane nodded to her as she approached the bus stop.

"Hey," she answered back.

"I'm sorry," they said at the same time, stopping when they realized the other was speaking, too. Then, as if rehearsed, they did it again. "Go ahead."

They both laughed.

"So... you had a good chemistry lesson with Kate?"

"So... you didn't tell your parents yet, I take it?"

"This weather sucks." Joanie kicked a rock with her

toe and it skittered out into the street.

"If it clears up, you want to hit the cemetery after school?"

"Yes. Yeah." Joanie nodded, grateful that Zane was letting her off the hook for now.

"You really want to know about Kate?"

"I'm not blind, Zane, I know you like her."

"I do. She's pretty, she's funny, she's... well she's smart, though not so much in chemistry."

"No?"

"No, she's going to need, like, a real tutor I think, and not because she switched schools."

Joanie nodded. "I can relate."

"Joanie, are you really mad? I mean... I know you like her, too, and—"

"No, Zane, I'm not mad," Joanie interrupted. "I'm just a little bummed out, okay? I'm happy for you. I hope it works out."

"Yeah?"

"Yeah, of course, you idiot. It's not like I can make her like me." If she were another guy she might not give up so quickly, but Joanie really believed that you can't try to convince someone they want something they don't. If Kate was into guys, then there wasn't anything Joanie could really do about it. That was just life. No one would ever be able to convince Joanie that she didn't like girls, either.

"I do feel kinda bad, though." He did, Joanie could see it in his eyes. Zane was a smart guy, but he couldn't lie to Joanie about anything, she could always tell.

"Don't. It's cool. Really."

"Are you sure you don't need me to be your prom date?"

Joanie snorted. "No, Zane. Ask her."

Zane grinned at her, looking cute and shy. "I might."

"You should." Joanie smiled back.

"Hey, you look like you're freezing." Zane ducked under her umbrella with her and covered her bare, frozen fingers, which were wrapped around the handle, with his gloved ones. "Better?"

"Thanks, Zane. You're the best."

Their bus arrived a few minutes later and Joanie was just glad to be out of the rain.

By Friday, Kate was completely caught up in trig. Joanie didn't think she needed any more help, but Kate asked at lunch if she had time and Joanie agreed. They met at the library as usual, but when she opened the door for Kate, Kate just grinned at her, her blue eyes flashing.

"What?"

"I don't need to study," Kate said.

"Oh. Well, okay then. I guess I'll see you in trig later." Joanie was a little miffed though; she could have gone to the art room or something to hang out.

"Wait though. I asked you for a reason." Kate stuck out her hand and rested it on Joanie's arm. "Come on."

Joanie blinked at Kate, but followed along. "Where are we going?"

"I have something to give you. It's in my locker."

Kate's locker was in a completely different wing than Joanie's and they walked along quietly, not talking at all. Joanie had tried to be all business with Kate and not let on that she was feeling jealous, so they hadn't really talked about much besides math and school stuff. Silence sometimes made Joanie uncomfortable, but it didn't seem to with Kate, kind of like how it wasn't weird with Zane either.

When they got to Kate's locker, Kate smiled at Joanie and opened it. "I wanted to give you something to say thank you for your help this week. Well, for that and just... because you've been really nice to me."

Joanie was surprised. "Oh, Kate, you didn't have to--"

"Here." Kate held her hands out toward Joanie. In them was a small box that was covered in overlapping layers of colorful paper.

"Oh, wow. This is so pretty," Joanie said, taking the box. She turned it over in her fingers and something slid around inside.

"It's decoupage. It was just a plain little box, but I took some tissue paper and some glue and..." Kate shrugged. "Well, anyway. Open it up."

Joanie opened the box and inside was a pair of beaded earrings. They had silver ear hooks, a couple of small translucent blue beads that were kind of pyramid shaped, and in between them was a neat fish-shaped bead that was the same color blue.

"Oh, wow," Joanie said, taking one out of the box. "Did you make these?"

"I did, yes. Do you like them?" Kate bit her lip.

"I love them!" Joanie put the box back into Kate's hands and then took off the earrings she'd worn that day, trading them for the fish. "How do they look?"

Kate looked back at her, smiling in a way that made Joanie melt inside. "Beautiful."

Joanie smiled back, hoping it didn't show. "Thank you so much."

"You're welcome."

"That's so cool that you make jewelry. How do you keep track of all those tiny beads? I'd lose them all over the place."

"It's not that hard, actually." Kate's blue eyes met Joanie's and Joanie felt her heart skip a beat. "I could show you sometime."

"I... I'd like that."

She knew she was blushing. Joanie was glad suddenly that their tutoring sessions were over. She didn't think she could handle this anymore. She'd end up saying something to Kate that she shouldn't. Zane was one lucky guy, that was for sure.

She and Kate had to go their separate ways for the next period, but Joanie fiddled with her earrings and couldn't really concentrate in class for the rest of the afternoon.

It had stopped raining by the time school let out, and Joanie and Zane hung out in a patch of warm sun, leaning up against a headstone in one of the older parts of the cemetery. The town they lived in was old; there were plaques on the outside of a couple of the buildings on Main Street that said "Washington slept here". This part of the cemetery wasn't quite that old, but the headstones were worn and unreadable in places and many of them were covered in yellow and green moss.

She and Zane knew all of the names by heart, at least the ones in this little section of the graveyard, and they'd made up all kinds of stories about how the people had lived and died, how they knew each other, even what they did for a living.

They were leaning against the oversized plot marker for the family "Truhern". Owen Truhern, Joanie had decided a couple of years ago, had been a carpenter, and his wife, Alice, had given him four sons. There were only markers for three of the sons, however, because the fourth son, according to Zane, had run off with the daughter of a blacksmith before he turned eighteen, never to be seen by his family again.

The rest of the Truhern sons had gone on to lead interesting lives, if Zane and Joanie's rendition of history was to be believed. Alex Truhern had always been a wild kid. He was a bully in school and used to beat up his older brothers and make his mother cry. He robbed at bank in broad daylight at the age of twenty-six and was killed as he was fleeing the sheriff. The sheriff was a good shot.

Daniel Truhern became a librarian and never married. There were rumors about him; rumors that he'd drank too much and ate bugs, rumors that he wore women's clothing when he was alone in the library at night and that he would follow people home just to see where they lived. While people liked to make things up about him and believe them, none of the rumors was true at all. He was just a nice man who really liked books.

The eldest son, Richard Truhern, was a tall, handsome fellow who married a nice girl and had two daughters. He was always very into debate and politics growing up and was eventually elected Mayor. That part about Richard was actually true; it said so on his gravestone. What it didn't say, however, was just how much money Richard had embezzled while in office. And it didn't mention all the chocolate he bought with it to soothe his addiction. It was shocking, really.

The Truherns had been silent witnesses to many a private conversation between Joanie and Zane. Today, they were getting another earful.

"So, how do I say it? I mean, just blurting it out over dinner seems like a pretty lame idea."

"I don't know, Jo. I guess you could sit them both down..."

"Or I could tell my mom first."

"Or your dad maybe?"

"Hmm. Maybe."

"I'm sorry, Jo, I know it's really hard."

Joanie nodded. It was hard. It was maybe the hardest thing she'd ever done. Telling Zane had been so easy; he just shrugged and started pointing out cute girls. Her dad wasn't going to do that.

"Maybe I'll tell Liz. She can't keep a secret."

Zane chuckled at her. "That would be very sneaky and very chicken of you."

"I guess."

She wanted to tell them. She wanted them to know who she was and to understand her. She wasn't ashamed of who she was or anything, never had been. She wasn't even afraid of the kids at school; she just... didn't like taking risks if she didn't have to.

She hadn't even told Zane about the earrings or the little box that Kate had made for her.

"So have you asked Kate to the prom yet?" Joanie asked, changing the subject.

"Not yet, I was thinking next week. Seems kind of lame to ask her when I've only known her a week, you know?"

"Well, you better ask her before someone else does. Pretty new girl and all."

Zane looked at Joanie. "Oh, yeah. Good idea."

"And you're not the only handsome guy in our class,

you know," Joanie joked.

"Yeah, I am."

Joanie gave Zane a shove and he fell over, right onto Owen Truhern.

"So," Zane asked, sitting up again. "You're going to tell them?

"Yeah, soon." Joanie nodded, still trying to convince herself it was a good idea. "And you're going to ask her?"

Zane nodded. "Yeah. Soon."

CHAPTER SEVEN

Joanie slept late on Saturday. Very late. She told herself she was just tired, but she wasn't even fooling herself. She knew she was hiding.

It was time to talk to her parents, and she'd decided to start with her dad. He spent his Saturdays working on the house; mowing, weeding, fixing things. He was always tinkering in the garage on Saturday afternoons, rewiring something or building shelves for the basement, anything that kept his hands busy.

When she finally got out of bed it was nearly lunchtime so she took a quick shower, pulled on her favorite comfy outfit and decided to bring her dad a sandwich. Maybe he'd take it all better on a full stomach.

"Hey you, is that for me?" Her dad smiled at her and picked up a rag to clean off his hands.

"Yep. Tinkering is hungry work, I hear."

"I'll have you know I'm finally getting around to putting together that cabinet thing for the upstairs bathroom so you can finally stop complaining that there's nowhere to put your stuff."

"Wow, you must really be desperate for something to do," Joanie joked, making them both laugh.

"So, how did the test go yesterday?"

"Chem? Eh. Okay, I guess. I'm pretty sure I passed."

"Knew you would. You think you'll make honor roll again this semester?"

"Looks like." Joanie nodded. She was grateful for that anyway; she'd hate to have to say 'hey Dad, I'm gay *and* I missed the honor roll'. He might have a heart attack or something.

"Great. So, listen, I was thinking maybe we'd go looking for a car for your birthday."

Joanie jumped. "...what?"

"You'll be getting your license in May right?"

"Well, yeah, but..."

"Well, you're certainly not going to drive *my* car."

Joanie grinned at what she knew was her dad's way of getting the car idea past her mother. "Oh! Well, no. Of course not."

"Of course not." Her dad took a bite of his sandwich. "Mmm. Delicious."

"Dad... I uh," Joanie's resolve faltered a little after the talk about honor roll and the car. Zane was right; she didn't like disappointing her parents at all.

"Don't worry, we'll take care of the insurance. But you'll have to pay for your own gas, okay?"

"Oh. Yeah, okay. That's... cool. Great. Thank you."

Her dad nodded, chewing. "Something else on your mind?" he asked.

Joanie shook her head. "Uh, no." Tomorrow. She'd tell him tomorrow. "No. Nope. Just thought you might like a sandwich."

"Thanks."

"Yep. Uh... yeah. See you later."

Joanie didn't tell him on Sunday either. She just couldn't find the right words, and let several more weeks go by without telling anyone anything at all. The prom was just over a month away now, she didn't have a date, and, until she told her parents, she wasn't going to get one either. Not to mention that her school was full of straight girls, and at this point, she wasn't sure she could find a date anyway.

Meanwhile, Zane and Kate were still hanging out, and working on chemistry together. They'd meet every day at X-period, when she and Kate used to meet for math. One Friday after school, Zane seemed upset about something and slouched in his seat on the bus ride home.

Joanie poked him in the arm. "What's up?"

"Nothing." Zane sighed.

"Zane..."

"Nothing."

"Is it Kate?"

Zane nodded. "I guess I waited too long."

"You what?"

"I waited too long and someone else asked her to the

prom."

"Oh, no. Oh, Zane, I'm sorry."

"I should have spoken up sooner, I just… it didn't seem, I don't know, gentlemanly or something to ask a girl to a prom that you barely know. She'd have thought it was just because of her looks or something. She never would have believed that I actually liked *her*."

Zane was the sweetest guy in the world. He thought so hard about other people's feelings that that he just waited himself out of a prom date. The last time Zane looked the way he did right now, Samantha had just dumped him. He shook his head and crossed his arms over his chest.

Joanie patted his shoulder. "Who is she going with?"

"She wouldn't tell me."

"That sucks, Zane. I'm really sorry."

"You have a date yet?"

"No."

"Well if you don't get one…"

"If I don't, and at this point I don't think I will, of course I'll go with you, Zane."

"Okay. Thanks Joanie." He looked over at her. "You're the only girl that's never let me down, you know that?"

Joanie smiled. "And I'm not about to start."

Well, if nothing else she'd be off the hook for telling her parents anything for a little while longer.

It was Saturday again, and Joanie was sitting in the kitchen when the phone rang. Liz answered it.

"Hello? Yeah, she actually got out of bed this morning."

"Shut up, brat!"

"Hang on," she said into the receiver and then handed

it to Joanie. "Here you go, Sleeping Beauty."

You are so dead, Joanie mouthed at Liz, who pretended to shake with fear and then stuck out her tongue.

"Hello?"

"Hi Joanie, it's Kate."

"K... Kate?" Joanie stammered. "Uh. Hi, how are you?" Kate was the last person Joanie would have expected a phone call from.

"I'm okay. Sorry to bug you."

"No, no you're not. Um... let me just go upstairs."

"No, wait, Joanie, this is just really quick. I mean, I do want to talk, but not over the phone. Can you hang out today?"

"Uh, sure. When?"

"Well, I was thinking maybe we could get something to eat."

"Okay." Perfect. Joanie had a craving anyway. "How about pizza?"

"Sounds good. Meet you downtown at, like, noon?"

"Noon is good, yeah. At Vinny's. You know where that is?"

"Sure do. Thanks, Joanie. See you there."

"Bye."

Joanie hung up the phone. She had a feeling she knew what Kate wanted to talk about. It was probably about Zane and what was going on with him. Joanie figured at the very least she'd find out who Kate's prom date was. Maybe she could even get Kate to change her mind. Poor Zane had been pretty upset; maybe Kate didn't realize how he felt about her. Maybe she'd have said yes if she had known.

***

Spring was coming on slowly this year and it was a chilly bike ride into town, but Joanie didn't mind it. She liked biking and did it a lot to get around. It'd be cool when she got a car, but for now this was just fine. She dressed casually in jeans and a warm sweater, and decided on just a light windbreaker over that. It was already starting to warm up outside.

Joanie got to Vinny's before Kate did, locked her bike up and went inside.

Vinny's was a town institution. There were other places you could get pizza that were bigger or newer or part of a popular chain, but as far as Kate was concerned, there was really nowhere else that anyone would get their pizza if they knew how good Vinny's was. It looked kind beat up from the outside, old, with a plain glass front. It had Formica-covered booths inside and a scratched up linoleum floor. But it always smelled like heaven.

She found a booth off to one side away from the widows where it would be less drafty and sat down to wait for Kate.

A sleek sports car pulled up a few minutes later and Kate climbed out. Joanie watched as Kate showed the driver her cell phone and waved before the car drove away. Kate spotted Joanie as soon as she came in, and smiled.

Joanie was still having dreams about that smile. And Kate's blue, blue eyes.

"Hi!" Kate said, pulling her coat off before sitting down. She blew on her fingers to warm them. "Man, it's really cold out there."

"You're kidding, right? I thought you were the tough-skinned Chicago girl?"

"I didn't say that. Cold is cold!"

Joanie laughed. "Want to go order?"

"Yeah." Kate looked around. "We go up to the counter?"

"Uh-huh. Vinny doesn't have wait staff."

"Vinny is an actual person?"

"Oh, yeah. He's an ancient guy who makes amazing pizza."

"Cool."

They got up and made their way to the counter, leaving their stuff in the booth. Joanie never worried about her stuff here. She and Zane spent so much time here after school it practically felt like home.

"What can I get you ladies?"

It wasn't Vinny behind the counter, it was George, who Joanie knew was related to Vinny, but she had no idea how.

"Hey George, can I get a small calzone with meatballs and mushrooms?"

"Small calzone, meatballs and mushrooms. And what for you?" George asked with a thick accent. He looked at Kate, who was still perusing the menu that was posted on a large board over George's head.

"Um... a chicken parm sub, please?"

"Have a seat ladies, I call you when is ready."

Kate looked at Joanie, and Joanie smiled and nodded at her. "We pay after."

"Wow, the honor system."

"No one would dare rip Vinny off. He might break your legs."

"Ohh..." Kate's eyes grew wide.

"No! No, no, I'm kidding!" Joanie laughed. "Totally kidding."

"Hey, I'm from Chicago, we don't joke about things

like that." Kate said seriously, then she winked and gave Joanie a smile.

"Heh. I suppose you don't."

They each got Cokes and then they sat down again. Kate slid into her side of the booth and sat on her fingers.

"You want my gloves?" Joanie offered.

"Nah, I'm good."

"So, was that your dad?" Joanie asked before sipping her coke.

"My mom."

"She drives a nice car."

Kate shrugged. "I guess. It's small."

"So how do you think you did on the English test yesterday?"

"Awesome. Thank you so much for your help."

"You're welcome." Joanie shifted in her seat, trying to look casual as she steered the conversation toward Zane. "How's chemistry going?"

"Oh, fine. Fine." Kate shrugged again. "I don't really like it, but Zane's been a big help."

"Well that's good I guess. You guys are hanging out together a lot, huh?"

"Just to study."

Joanie smiled. "That's it? Studying?"

Kate nodded. "Sure. I mean, it's not like he's not a nice guy and all, I totally see why he's your best friend, but it's just studying."

Joanie smiled, but inside she felt kind of bad for Zane. Kate obviously wasn't as interested in him as he was in her, and she had a feeling that Kate would have turned Zane down even if she didn't hadn't accepted someone else's invitation to the prom.

"So you don't like him, huh? I mean, *like him* like him?"

Kate sighed. "No. I feel bad; I know I disappointed him. Did he tell you?"

"About the prom? Yeah."

Kate nodded. "He was cool about it, but I still felt bad."

"So who are you going with?"

"I don't know yet."

Joanie raised an eyebrow. "Oh? He got the impression that you were already going with someone else." Joanie leaned one arm on the table.

"Yeah. I thought saying that I was going with someone else sounded better than saying I just didn't want to go with him."

"Oh." Joanie winced. Poor Zane. "I guess so, yeah."

Their food arrived and the conversation ended suddenly as they both started eating.

"Oh, my God, this is good."

"Yummy, right? This place is the best."

"It's hard to beat Chicago for pizza but this is a really good chicken parm. Wow."

Joanie dug into her calzone and ate every bite of it. It was cheesy and the meatballs were spicy and it was exactly what the doctor ordered. She was completely stuffed by the time she finished. "I ate that whole thing, man. I'm disgusting." She grinned.

Kate laughed and then groaned. "Me too. I won't need dinner tonight that's for sure. It was so good though."

"You want to take a walk and digest a little?"

"Why? Can't I nap here?" Kate grinned and tilted her head, making a sleepy gesture. Joanie knew how she felt. She was always in food coma when she left Vinny's.

"Vinny kind of frowns on sleeping in his booths." Joanie said completely deadpan, then slid out of the booth and stood up. "Zane fell asleep while we were doing homework once and Vinny dumped ice water on him." She laughed when Kate did, which only made her feel fuller. "Oh, man, I can barely move." She pulled her wallet out of her pocket.

"Wait, wait. I got it." Kate put a hand on Joanie's to stop her and stood up. "I'll be right back."

"Kate, you don't have to--"

"Hush up. I am," Kate said, waving a hand as she crossed the restaurant to the cash register.

Joanie looked at her wallet and then put it back in her pocket. She couldn't be sure, but paying for lunch was kind of a date thing, wasn't it? She'd never really had a *real* date so she couldn't be sure, but Zane said he always paid when he took girls out.

"All set." Kate handed Joanie some mints. "George sent these to you, says the meatballs are garlicky."

"Oh, they were. And so yummy!" Joanie grinned, popping a mint into her mouth.

"I have to be home by five," Kate said, pulling on her coat. "We have some family thing tonight."

"Saturdays are spaghetti night at my house." Joanie rolled her eyes at herself. She'd just eaten a half a ton of calzone, she wasn't going to need more Italian food tonight. She tucked her scarf around her neck and pulled her shell over her head.

"Does your mom make garlic bread?" Kate asked her.

"I eat more of that than I do the spaghetti!"

"With cheese on it?"

"Yep. It's awesome."

"Can I come over one Saturday?" Kate grinned broadly. "Please?"

Joanie laughed.

It was still kind of chilly out, but she and Kate walked through town looking in shop windows and poking their heads into a couple of the clothing stores. They spent a good long while in the bookstore, too. Kate bought a brass bookmark and a desk calendar, and Joanie bought a new blank book and a couple of nice pens. They were just deciding whether they should stop in at the coffee shop for some hot cocoa when Kate's cell phone rang.

"Hello? Yeah, hi, Dad." She crossed her eyes at Joanie and Joanie laughed. Kate was so funny and so cool to hang out with. "Okay, I'll see you there. Yes, Dad, I'm going now, okay? Geez. Bye."

Joanie bumped shoulders with her. "Headed home?"

"Yeah, Dad says to meet him at the library."

"Perfect, my bike is back that way by Vinny's anyway. I'll walk over with you."

They took a few steps, but then Kate's voice stopped Joanie. "Wait."

"What's up?" Joanie squinted at Kate, noticing that it was starting to get dark out.

"I, uh... Joanie, I was wondering if maybe..."

"Yeah?"

Kate sighed and shrugged. "You know what, never mind."

"What?"

"Nothing, come on. My dad is gonna be pissed if I'm late."

Kate's dad showed up in an SUV and took Kate home.

Joanie watched the car pull away still trying to figure out what Kate had decided not to say to her. Giving up, she rode her bike home in the dark. She had lights and a helmet, but still her mom seemed all worried when she got home.

She managed to avoid a confrontation with her mother about it until dinner time. She wasn't at all hungry, but her parents' rule was that everyone sat at the table during dinner whether they were eating or not.

"I don't like you riding in the dark." Her mother started in on Joanie as soon as she arrived in the kitchen.

"I was careful, mom. Geez."

"Still. What if someone hit you?"

"Nobody hit me."

"That's not the point, Joanie." Her mom sighed and finished putting a plate together.

"The point is you worry way too much, mom. I'm sixteen! I can ride my damn bike home from town."

"Don't you talk to me like that, young lady."

"Fine. Sorry." She sank into a chair and crossed her arms over her chest. Her mom sat a huge plate of spaghetti with homemade meatballs and a slice of cheesy garlic bread in front of her. "Oh God, mom. I had a calzone at Vinny's. I'm so not hungry."

"Just eat a little something, you grouch."

"'M not grouchy." Joanie felt like sulking, but she wasn't sure why. She thought maybe it had something to do with Kate, but Kate had been so nice to her. What could the problem be?

Beside her, Liz laughed. "Grouchy."

"Shut up, squirt."

Liz stuffed her mouth with spaghetti.

Joanie ate a few bites of spaghetti and all of the bread

but the longer she sat there, the more she wanted to go away. Escape to her room and write, draw, work things out. Think about what was up with Kate.

"That sound okay, Joanie?"

Joanie blinked, looking up from her dinner. "Huh?"

"Oh, honey, are you tired? You look tired."

"A little. Sorry. What did you ask me?"

"Your mom said she signed you up for some driver's instruction before you take the road test in May."

"Oh," Joanie nodded. "Yeah, awesome. Thanks."

"I was saying maybe you and I could go for a drive this weekend. Teach you a few things."

Joanie nodded. She'd had her permit for a month and had only been out driving a few times. "Sounds great, Dad."

"Joanie, honey, why don't you head up to bed?" Her mom put a hand on Joanie's forehead, and Joanie rolled her eyes.

"I'm not sick, Mom."

"Well? I just wanted to be sure."

Liz slurped down the last bite of spaghetti on her plate. "May I please be excused?" she asked hastily. Joanie knew she wanted to go watch TV.

"Of course. Take your plate to the sink. Joanie, you head on upstairs. I'll come check on you in a little while." Joanie's mom took her plate for her.

"Thanks, Mom," she looked at her dad. "And you, too, Dad," she winked. Joanie was starting to think that her dad was almost as excited about Joanie learning to drive as Joanie was herself.

Joanie's room was a mess, but it was her sanctuary. It was cluttered with a mix of things from her childhood, holidays, vacations, you name it. She had a beat up, loved-on, stuffed cow that played a lullaby when you wound it up from when she was two. Her first pair of Converse high-tops, long outgrown, hung from the light fixture overhead. She loved to read and she had books on shelves, on the floor, and stacked on her desk. There was a shelf that held nothing but her old journals. She had stickers on the full length mirror on the back of her bedroom door, a poster of David Bowie on the wall, a ton of CDs in a tall rack, a small TV in one corner, and two twin beds with plain red comforters. The bed she slept in had loads of pillows; she loved pillows, even though most of them ended up on the floor by morning.

She tossed the new journal and the pens she'd bought in town on the spare bed. On the nightstand was her current journal, filled with ramblings and sketches and other private thoughts. She flopped on her bed and opened it, grabbing the pen that was lying next to it. She pulled out the postcard she was using for a bookmark – Zane had sent it to her from the Grand Canyon last summer – and started to write.

Kate

Just her name, and then again in all caps:

KATE

Joanie tapped the pen on her chin. Kate turned Zane down for the prom even though she didn't have another date. She bought Joanie lunch. She started to say something today, something important, and then changed her mind. All of these things had to mean something. What had Kate been going to say? Joanie started scribbling.

Can I borrow five dollars?

Are you doing anything tomorrow night?

Do you like me?

She circled the last question and surrounded it with

question marks. Then, as she often did when she was thinking about someone, she started to sketch.

The first frame was Kate, hair down, falling around her face and lit with sunlight. She was smiling, her eyes shining, and she was looking at something. Or someone.

People in Joanie's journal were always cartoonish, as if out of a comic strip. Features that Joanie particularly liked about people were usually out of proportion to make them stand out. In Kate's case, her eyes were a bit large, but her smile was larger and full of teeth.

In the second frame was Joanie in her usual cartoon state, a little cross-eyed with her short-ish hair curling and lifting away from her head like it was being blown in the wind. She was looking back toward frame one, cartoon Kate, with a raised eyebrow.

Frame three was a thought bubble that led to an off-screen speaker. Even as she drew it, Joanie wasn't sure who was speaking. In the bubble were the words, "Are you like me?"

It could easily have been Joanie, but it might well have been Kate.

Kate + Joanie

The names looked good together. Her little cartoon versions of Kate and Joanie looked good together, too.

If Kate *were* gay, that would explain treating for lunch, and turning down a cutie like Zane for the prom. The idea that Kate might be interested in her made Joanie's chest ache a little. It felt familiar, like something she'd felt there before.

A little like fear.

What if Kate did like her? What if Kate wanted to date her? Joanie got a little nervous thinking about it. It wasn't a huge school, people would find out soon enough, then her parents would find out, her teachers... then she'd be living life Out. Out. What a scary concept. But there was no question that Joanie had a crush on Kate. A big, huge, undeniable, obvious crush.

Crush, was the next word that Joanie wrote down in her journal. She hadn't had a real crush since eighth grade when she thought Amy Wilson was the prettiest girl she'd ever seen. She'd never told Amy about it, or anyone else for that matter, she just watched Amy in class and in the lunchroom and drew pictures in her journal. She had wanted to kiss Amy so badly that she used to practice on her pillow. It was the first time that Joanie had ever wanted to kiss anyone at all, boy or girl, and after that, the things she'd been thinking and feeling since about fourth grade made much more sense.

That was when she figured out that she liked girls.

She'd been so excited to finally understand who she was and what was going on that she ran right out and told Zane.

"No way, really?" Zane had asked her, his eyes wide and his blond hair a mess and sticking out in a hundred directions like it still did now. She'd drawn that in her journal, too. Zane, with gigantic eyes. "Cool. You're the only gay person I know."

Zane hadn't meant that statement to worry her, she knew that now. He'd meant that she was unique and he liked that about her. But she didn't understand that then, and that night in bed, the part of Joanie that just wanted to be like everyone else, that just wanted to be normal, that part won, and Joanie decided not to tell her parents anything. In fact, to this day she'd never told anyone but Zane.

The next thing she knew she'd drawn her cartoon dad

with his balding head and his argyle golf vest and socks, and her cartoon mom with her knitting needles and her hair in a bun. Joanie was scribbling cartoon pictures of herself telling her parents she was gay into her journal. But she had no idea how they were going to react, so for the moment, the faces in her drawing were all blank.

Including her own.

CHAPTER EIGHT

oanie, wait up!"

Joanie stopped on her way to the bus stop when Zane called her name.

"Hey, you're late!"

"I am not," Zane protested.

"Yes you are. You're usually here waiting by the time I get here."

"I'm not late, you're early, Jo."

Joanie looked at her watch. Zane was right, she was almost ten minutes earlier than usual. "Oh." Oops.

"Are we a little eager to get to school today?" Zane poked her in the shoulder.

"What? No." She didn't mean to sound defensive.

Zane shrugged. "Just weird to see you, is all. How was your weekend?"

"Oh," Joanie said casually. She knew Zane was going to ask; why hadn't she prepared herself? "Uh, well. You know, boring. Studied, went to the bookstore and bought a new journal."

"Had pizza with Kate."

Joanie stopped walking. "Uh, yeah."

"I stopped in for some pizza after work. George said you guys had just left. You and a long-haired girl..."

"You know, that might not have been Kate."

"But it was, and you didn't want to tell me."

Joanie had to think fast. In the end she decided on the truth, or at least what the truth had been when she first agreed to have lunch with Kate. "I was trying to find out who she was going to go to the prom with. I thought maybe I could get her to change her mind about going with you." Not a chance as it turned out.

Zane snorted, falling for her explanation completely. "Great, she's gonna think I asked you to--"

"No. Now come on, Zane, I'm smarter than that."

Zane nodded. "Yeah, okay. So, who is she going with?"

"Oh. She... wouldn't tell me, either." Joanie didn't lie to Zane very often. In fact she couldn't really remember the last time she had just outright lied to him. Hopefully she was better at it than he was.

"Oh." Zane shrugged. "Whatever. She's weird." He still seemed disappointed. Oh boy, what a mess this could turn out to be.

The bus arrived, saving Joanie from having to say anything more about it, which was good because she didn't really like lying to Zane.

Classes in the morning went pretty quickly. Joanie ran into Kate and Zane in math class and said hello to both but didn't hang out long with either of them. Kate, however, found Joanie in the library during X-period and sat down next to her.

Joanie looked up, startled. "Hi."

"Hi," Kate whispered to her. "Studying?"

"Reading. English homework," Joanie whispered back. She showed Kate her copy of *Pride and Prejudice*.

"Oh. Good book."

"Yeah. What's up?"

"I just wanted to say thanks for letting me buy you lunch on Saturday."

For letting me buy you lunch. See? There was something going on. There had to be. "Hey," Joanie smiled, watching Kate, trying to get a read on her. "Who doesn't like Vinny's?"

"I had a really good time." Kate smiled at her and Joanie felt that... *thing* again, the heartbeat thing and the warmth in her face.

"Me too," Joanie managed to say as casually as possible.

Kate nodded, then shifted in her seat. "I was... Well. I wanted to ask you something, but I'm a little... nervous about it."

Ask me out. Joanie thought. But all she said was, "Okay." Did she dare hope? Other than the lunch thing, she didn't really have any reason to believe that Kate liked her that way.

Kate looked around the library. "Can we go somewhere else?"

"Uh, yeah. Okay. Let me just get my stuff..." Joanie started putting her books back into her bag. Kate stood up and took a couple of slow steps toward the library doors, waiting. As soon as Joanie had her bag packed up, she followed Kate.

"Everything okay?" she asked.

Kate nodded. "Yeah, I just didn't feel like whispering this whole conversation." Kate stopped and peered into nearby a classroom. "Come on."

Joanie followed her into the empty classroom and watched as Kate closed the door.

"Kate, what's up? Is everything okay? You're kind of freaking me out now."

"Sorry." Kate said. "It's just that... Well. I really did have a good time on Saturday."

Joanie squinted at her. "I did, too. Really."

Kate took a step closer and clasped her hands in front of her. "And I was wondering if... do you know I'm gay?"

Joanie blinked. "I... didn't know that, no." But Joanie had been hoping. If the pounding of her heart meant anything she'd apparently been hoping a lot harder than she'd realized. "I didn't know."

"Okay. And now that you do, are you... *okay* with it?"

"I'm... *fine* with that." Glad. She was glad. Why didn't she just say so?

Kate nodded and smiled. "Great. That's... well. It's just that I'd like to... I try to be honest about it with my friends, you know? And if you're going to be my friend then you should know."

Joanie raised an eyebrow, trying to figure Kate out. "Friends?"

Kate seemed to get braver at Joanie's hint. "Unless, actually I was... what I wanted to ask you, and I tried on Saturday but there just wasn't enough time with my dad and all..."

"Yes?" *Go on, ask me. Ask me, ask me, ask me.* The picture Joanie had drawn of them in her journal looking at each other came to mind. It was definitely Joanie that had been asking the question, she realized now.

"I wanted to ask if you wanted to go to the movies this weekend," Kate asked in a rush. "Just the movies, it doesn't have to be--"

"Yes." Joanie jumped on the invitation. "Yes, I'd love to." Joanie smiled.

"Oh. Great." Kate exhaled in a loud whoosh and smiled back, just in time for the period bell to ring.

Chapter Nine

In all her years of high school, Joanie had never been on a real date.

She could have used Zane's advice about what to wear, and what she should and shouldn't talk about, but Zane still didn't know she was going out with Kate. Joanie was going to tell him, but she chickened out again and she decided she would wait and see how things went first. If it sucked and she and Kate never had another one, there would be nothing to talk about anyway.

But Joanie really didn't think it was going to suck.

She dressed up a little, as dressy as she ever got anyway, in a pair of black pants, low heels and the awesome funky blue blouse that Zane brought her from his trip with his parents to Germany last winter. Probably his mother had picked it out for him, but she knew the idea had been his at least.

She combed her hair and then put some waxy gunk in it to make it shiny, which also worked like a gel so she could style it, too. Her hair was short-ish, a lot shorter than

Kate's but not super short, either, and where Kate's had a natural curl to it, Joanie's was stick straight and couldn't hold a curl for more than an hour or so no matter what she put in it. Joanie had tried curling irons, hot rollers, sleeping on those twisty things, and then, exasperated, had given up on it all a long time ago and got a blunt cut that made her hair look more like she had straightened it on purpose.

Kate sent her a text message saying they were leaving the house and Joanie really got nervous, but she managed to find her wallet and her shoes and was downstairs on time. Zane would have been proud of her.

"You look nice, Joanie," her mother said with a questioning tone.

"Yeah, where are you going? You got a date or something?" Liz asked. Joanie wanted to kill her.

Her mom picked right up on that one. "A date?"

"Mom, I don't have a date. I'm just going to the movies with Kate."

"With just Kate?"

"Yes, Mom."

"Okay," her mom didn't seem to believe her, but she let it go, thankfully. "Well, keep your cell phone on. Be home by ten."

"Ten? Mom, it's a seven o'clock movie."

"Fine. Eleven."

"Midnight? Please?"

"Eleven, Jo."

Joanie sighed as Kate's mom pulled into the driveway and honked. "Fine. Bye."

"Hi," Kate said, getting out to move the front seat of

her mom's car so Joanie could climb into the backseat. Joanie was surprised but pleased when Kate slipped into the back with her. "Joanie, this is my mom. Mom, Joanie."

"Hello, Mrs. Dalton."

"Hello, Joanie." Mrs. Dalton looked at her in the rearview mirror and smiled before pulling out of Joanie's driveway. "Kate says you were very helpful getting her caught up in school, Joanie."

"Oh, it's no big deal."

"I think it's a bigger deal than you know. Thank you."

Joanie glanced at Kate. "Uh, okay. You're welcome."

"So what are you two seeing on your date?"

Joanie swallowed and felt herself go pale. Kate must have noticed.

"It's cool, Joanie, Mom knows about me."

"Uh. Oh. Okay, but..." Without asking, Kate had outed Joanie to her mom, and Joanie felt herself starting to panic inside.

Kate looked at her, as if reading her mind. "You're... not out at all? Your parents don't know?"

Joanie shook her head, no.

Mrs. Dalton interrupted. "I won't tell anyone, Joanie. Don't you worry, hon."

Joanie nodded and forced herself to breathe again as Kate patted her knee. Kate's mom seemed cool about it, and she believed Mrs. Dalton when she said she wouldn't tell anyone. Once Joanie managed to calm down, she realized she was maybe a little bit jealous. She'd like for her mom to know and be cool about it, too. Trouble was Joanie had no idea how her mom was going to react really. It would probably be okay in the end, but at first...

well, Joanie envied Kate a little.

She caught another look from Mrs. Dalton in the rear view mirror and blushed, but Mrs. Dalton just smiled and gave her a wink. Maybe this was okay after all. Kate's mom was driving them to their date, Kate's hand was resting on her knee, and Joanie smiled. Yeah. This was okay.

They got out of the car and went into the Chinese restaurant, which was right next door to the movie theater.

Joanie thanked Mrs. Dalton for the ride and hurried inside. Kate jogged after her. "I'm so sorry, Joanie, I kind of tell my mom everything."

Joanie nodded. "It's okay. I should, too, but... I don't know. I tried to tell my dad, but I just... didn't. I'm sort of..." She shrugged.

"Worried they're not going to like it?"

Joanie nodded. "I don't know. I kind of think they might be okay with it actually, I just... don't think they need to know yet."

"They don't need to?"

"Well, no. Not until there's a reason, you know? When there is a reason, I'll tell them."

"What kind of reason? I mean, what would be a reason they'd need to know?"

Joanie looked at Kate thinking, *you, maybe*, but she didn't say that. "I'm not sure yet. I'll know."

Kate watched her, looking into her eyes for a long time before speaking again. "Okay. It's cool, Joanie." Kate smiled at her. "I'm just glad you're here."

Joanie felt herself blush again.

A man interrupted them. "Table for two?"

"Yes, please," Kate answered smoothly. Joanie followed behind feeling strange.

"So, okay, you're not out at school, but... Zane knows, right?" Kate asked after they sat down.

Joanie nodded. "Oh, yeah. Zane has known forever."

"What's forever?"

"Since we were in, like, eighth grade."

Kate nodded. "Who else?"

"Nobody."

"Nobody at all?"

"Nope. People just don't..."

"Need to know."

"Yes. Right. They don't need to know." Joanie looked down at her menu. She could feel Kate's stare. It felt disapproving, almost worse than Joanie's mother's when Joanie said something her mother didn't like.

"Wow," Kate said finally. "That's got to be... hard."

Joanie blinked and looked up at Kate, not seeing any disapproval at all. Instead, Kate's eyes were soft with sympathy. Joanie shrugged.

"No, really. I mean, don't you want to be... you?"

"I am me."

"No, I mean, all the time. Aren't you kind of lonely?"

Joanie shrugged again.

"Well, if you need help, or want to talk, or... whatever..."

"Thanks. What are you eating?"

"Hmm." Kate looked down at her menu, letting Joanie change the subject.

"I'm thinking about sushi. They do sushi here, too."

"Yeah?" Kate flipped over her menu and looked at the back. "Oh, cool."

"Do you want to split a few things?"

"That'd be great. California roll?"

"Okay, "Joanie agreed. "How about edamame?"

"Excellent. Tuna?"

"Tuna sashimi, maybe?"

"Sure."

They agreed on everything they wanted to order as easily as she and Zane would have, and Joanie felt herself starting to relax. They didn't talk any further about being out, or even being gay, they just talked; about school, about bands they liked, about the movie they were going to see. They talked about shopping and books. They talked about Zane, and Joanie told some stories that made Kate laugh.

Kate's smile was still so amazing to Joanie. Bright and real and honest. She just laughed at things and told the truth and seemed so comfortable being herself. Joanie was drawn to it. Mesmerized by it. She wanted to learn how to be like that.

They almost walked out in the middle of the movie, but they made themselves wait until the end, if only because they'd paid for the tickets and they kept hoping it would get better.

"That sucked," Kate said as they were leaving the theater. Joanie usually stayed through all the credits, especially these days when you were never sure if there was going to be outtakes or extra footage at the end. But neither of them cared tonight, as it was possibly the worst movie they'd ever seen.

"I'm so sorry you wasted your money buying me a ticket," Joanie said, laughing as they hurried out the theater doors. The days were getting warmer but the nights were still cool and a whoosh of cold air blew Joanie's hair into her face. "Oh, man. Should've brought a jacket."

Kate's arm wrapped around her shoulders.

Joanie smiled and leaned into her warmth for a second but then remembered herself. "Thanks, but... not here, okay?" she asked, and pulled away. She took a couple of steps away and heard Kate sigh behind her.

"Fine."

Joanie stopped but didn't look at Kate. "I'm sorry."

"I understand, Joanie. It's okay."

"But you don't like it."

"No. But I like you. Come on, let's get on the bus, Mom can pick us up in town."

The bus was packed and bright and they were jostled and elbowed all the way back to town. Joanie looked at her phone. It was only ten. "I've got an hour," she told Kate as they stepped off the bus.

"Cool."

"Let's go inside someplace."

Kate pointed to the coffee shop and Joanie nodded.

They were quiet as they ordered, and Joanie insisted on buying for herself this time.

"I'm really sorry I freaked out on you back there," she told Kate as they found two comfortable seats.

"You didn't freak out." Kate smiled. "A freak out would have been, like, yelling at me and waving your arms or bursting into tears or something."

Joanie snorted. "Still. I wasn't very nice. I guess I'm... just not there yet, you know?"

"It's okay, Joanie. Don't worry about it." Kate sipped her cocoa and then took a huge bite out of the chocolate chip cookie she'd bought.

"How long have you been out?"

Kate looked at Joanie. "Um," she said with her mouth full, chewing her cookie quickly so she could answer.

"Oh, sorry!" Joanie laughed.

Kate waved her hand and swallowed. "I came out to my parents when I was twelve. But I knew long before that?"

"Really?"

"Yeah, I was maybe eight I think. I had a huge crush on a girl in my class. She had blonde hair and big green eyes and she was so pretty. I wanted to be her. I wanted to spend all my time with her. I just... knew."

"Wow."

"You haven't known that long?"

"No, I figured it out when I was thirteen. I might have known something was up before that, since about fourth grade I guess, but I had no idea what it was or what to call it."

Kate nodded. "Yeah, I hear you."

"How did you...?"

"Come out?"

"Yeah."

Kate laughed. "Well, I remember spending, like, half of seventh grade depressed because I'd decided I really wanted to tell people, but I didn't know how. And then finally one night, I figured it out."

"Yeah?" Joanie sipped her tea.

"Yeah. I figured my parents couldn't be mad at me if I was crying, right? So I sat on my bed and thought of every single sad thing I could. I thought about my cat that had been run over by a car, the day my grandma died, how I felt when I didn't get the part I wanted in the school play… and I just made myself cry."

"No way!"

Kate grinned. "And then I ran into my parent's bedroom and I threw myself into my mother's arms as dramatically as possible and I said 'Mom, I have to tell you something,' with tears streaming down my face."

Joanie sat on the edge of her seat. "And did she buy it?"

"Well, she told me I should wait for my dad to get out of the shower and tell them together, so I sat on the bed with her. I kept thinking 'keep crying, Kate. Keep crying,' and my mom kept looking at me funny. I gave up on trying to cry finally because the harder I tried, the more it kept making me laugh instead."

Joanie laughed with Kate. "Did your mom know already?"

"Yeah, I told them, and she was like, 'I kind of thought so.'"

"And your dad?"

"Oh, no. Dad had no idea. None. I think he was pretty shocked."

"Uh-oh," Joanie bit her lip.

"He came around in a few days."

"And how did you feel the next day?"

"The next day was the best day of my whole life!" Kate grinned broadly. "Oh, my God, it was like a whole new world out there. I told freakin' everybody. I didn't care what they thought. I was a new person. I felt free."

Joanie grinned, too, feeling happy for Kate. "Cool."

Kate nodded. "It was. You'll see."

Joanie nodded and Kate fed her bites of cookie. It was probably good they they'd gotten it all out of their systems now, so that next time they could just have a normal 'date' and not be so caught up in all the drama.

Joanie smiled to herself, already thinking about next time.

Kate called her mom at 10:30 p.m. and they stood outside in the chilly air waiting for Mrs. Dalton to pick them up. Joanie let Kate put her arm around her shoulders on the car ride home and she never once caught sight of Mrs. Dalton looking in the mirror. All she'd asked was, "Did you girls have a good time?" and otherwise, she hadn't said a thing.

Neither had Kate, who just held Joanie against her while Joanie rested her head on Kate's shoulder. It was nice. Really, really nice. So nice that Joanie was sorry to get home.

She hugged Kate in the car and slid out, and Kate climbed over the armrest into the front seat.

"'Night, Kate. Thank you," she said.

"It was fun! Think about next weekend," Kate called out the window as her mother pulled out of the driveway.

It was 11:05 p.m. when Joanie walked in the door. Her mom and dad were sitting on the couch watching TV, her mom was leaning into her dad's shoulder just like Joanie had been leaning on Kate in the car.

"Goodnight," Joanie said as she walked by, headed to her room.

"You're late," her father called out as she headed up the stairs. Joanie rolled her eyes.

CHAPTER TEN

Joanie sat in the driver's seat of the beige Toyota Corolla, both hands on the wheel, and looking straight ahead. She was excited about her first official driving lesson, but she was nervous, too.

"Okay, so I know this is boring and you think you know all of this stuff, but it's my job to make sure that you really do, so let's just run through it quickly and then we'll get to the fun part, okay?"

Joanie glanced at the instructor. He wasn't the old guy that Zane told her he'd had, with silver hair and bad breath. This guy was younger, kind of good looking even, and he was relaxed, slumping slightly in his seat. She shrugged at him. "You're the teacher."

"I'm Gary."

Joanie nodded, smiling. No 'Mr. so-and-so', this guy might be cool.

"Okay, Joanie. Use your directional indicator like you're going to turn right."

"My 'directional indicator'?" Joanie snorted. "You

mean my blinker?" Joanie clicked it over like she was turning right.

"I do, but the examiner at the DMV is going to call it a directional indicator. Indicate left, please."

Joanie moved the wand so it blinked left. "Geez. What does it matter what I call it as long as I know how to use it?"

"I completely agree. Turn that off and turn on your windshield wipers, please."

They went through wipers and headlights, then adjusted her seat and set her mirrors correctly, and they were off. Joanie had driven around the neighborhood with her dad a bunch of times so she knew those roads well. But Gary had her turn onto Euclid and head downtown.

"You sure you want to go downtown?" Joanie asked, a little skeptically. "There's lots of cars on a Saturday."

"Yep. That's my job, to take you places that are difficult to drive in."

Joanie shrugged. "It's your life," she joked, and turned left onto Main Street.

The straight drive down Main wasn't bad, just lots of stopping and going, lots of people pulling in and out of parking spaces and crossing the street. Joanie kept her eyes open and managed not to kill anyone. She was actually feeling pretty good about herself until she made the right hand turn onto Stedford and ran over the curb.

Gary shook his head at her. "Nope. Too tight, let's do that one again."

Joanie sighed.

"Hey, you want to impress your dates, don't you?"

Joanie snorted again.

"Okay, take the turn slow this time and try not to cut it so--"

Joanie hit the curb again. "Shit!" She gasped at her own outburst and then glanced at Gary, but he didn't seem to care about the swearing. "Sorry."

"You'll get it. One more time."

"Yeah, yeah."

Joanie went around the block and tried to make the turn a third time. This time, she eased right around the corner with no problem. "Ha!"

"Nice one. See?"

"Not bad. Cool. Maybe my date will be impressed after all."

"I'm sure he will."

"She."

"He, she, whatever. You'll be driving them all over town in a couple of months."

Joanie blinked. Had she just said that out loud? What the hell was she thinking? "Sorry."

Gary looked at her. "What did I miss? Did you forget your blinker or something?"

"I shouldn't have told you that."

"Told me what... oh. Why? Is there some new law that girls who date girls can't get a driver's license?"

"Uh. No? I guess not?" Joanie had no idea how to handle Gary's complete lack of reaction. "Where to now?"

"Let's head out to the mall."

Joanie drove to the end of Main Street and took the turn that went out toward the highway. "So you don't... care?"

"What, that you're gay? No. What does it have to do with me? I'm just supposed to make sure you don't crash the car." Gary grinned at her. "Just don't get distracted by the outfits some of those women at the mall wear, okay?"

Joanie laughed. "Oh, please."

The car went quiet for a few minutes, but now that Joanie had told someone, she just felt like talking.

"My parents don't know yet."

"I won't tell them," Gary promised. "Seriously. I'm here to teach you how to drive. Speaking of which, don't slam on the brakes, but that was our turn back there."

"Oh, shit!" Joanie slammed on the breaks. "Oh. Shit."

Gary reached over and took the wheel and they moved the car off the road. "It helps to listen while you talk."

"Sorry." Joanie knew she was sulking.

"Ah, ah, ah… none of that, now. We'll just get back on the road, take the next right and go around the block."

"Right. Sorry." Joanie was very careful pulling back into traffic and went around the block silently.

"So, are you going to tell them?" Gary asked as they pulled into the mall parking lot.

"Maybe? Yes. Eventually."

Gary nodded.

"Soon."

Gary shrugged. "I'm not saying you should or not, I was just asking."

"I'm going to. Soon. When I see how things go with Kate."

"Turn left into the lot over there." When Joanie parked the car in an empty spot, Gary continued. "Kate's your date?"

Joanie nodded. "But you don't really want to know all this stuff, do you?"

Gary shrugged. "Not if you don't want to tell me."

"She's new to the school. She's smart and pretty…"

"I'm a sucker for pretty girls, too."

Joanie smiled. "I'll tell my parents. I will. When they need to know."

"Okay, you're behind the wheel on that one."

Driving jokes. Joanie shook her head. "Boo."

"Hey, I'm just trying to do my job, here." Gary laughed.

The trip home went very smoothly, and Joanie was almost disappointed when it was over. "See you Thursday?"

"Thursday at," Gary pulled out his calendar. "Four o'clock. Oh, I'm picking you up at school this time." He grinned. "See you then."

"Bye."

CHAPTER ELEVEN

Joanie ran inside and changed into warmer clothes. Kate had called that morning to ask if Joanie wanted to go ice skating, and Joanie was so excited. She used to go a lot with Zane, but they hadn't been in ages, and it sounded like fun. It felt even more like a real date.

Early spring in New Jersey was always unpredictable. It was cold one minute and warm the next and tonight was going to be a cold one. She put thermals on under her jeans and shrugged into a sweater, then she went out to the garage to clean up her skates.

"Hey, you," her dad said as she came into the garage.

"Hey, Dad."

"Mom says you're going ice skating tonight?"

"Yeah, season's almost over, I know, but it sounded like fun."

"I'm sure it will be. I dug them out for you, they're over there."

"Oh, cool. Thanks, Dad." Joanie kissed him on the cheek as she walked by him and retrieved her skates.

"You look nice."

"Oh, uh. Thanks."

"Did your hair and all?"

"Not really, I just... messed with it a little to get it out of my face." Joanie sat down on a crate and took her skates out of their bag so she could clean them up.

"Who are you meeting?"

"Kate."

"And Zane?"

"Nope, not Zane tonight, Dad."

"Haven't seen him around much lately. I thought you guys were close?"

"We are, Dad, he's just... busy. I'm busy, that's all." She polished the boot in her hand a little more vigorously, trying to get it done faster so she could get out of there.

"Who is he taking to the prom?"

Oh, here we go again. Joanie sighed. "I don't know. No one yet as far as I know."

"Ah."

"Zane and I could go together, dad, but he really wants to find a real date."

"You're not a real date?"

"I'm not his girlfriend; we're just friends, okay? Just friends. Always been just friends. Geez." She switched to her other skate and started polishing that one quickly.

"Okay, okay. No need to get mad at me, I was just asking."

Joanie knew what was coming next. It was quiet for the thirty seconds that her father could stand waiting before he asked, "Do you have a date yet?"

Joanie sighed. "No. I'm still not sure if I even want to go."

"Do you know Liam Andrews?"

Joanie squinted up at her dad from where she was sitting on the crate. "...yeah, I know who Liam is." She had a bad feeling about this.

"Do you like him?"

"I don't know him, really, he's not in my section at school and he's not on my bus or anything."

Her father nodded. "He's looking for a date."

"Dad..."

"You know his father and I play golf together, right? Liam's a good kid. Good grades, polite, seems nice. Just think about it."

"Dad!"

"What? All I said was think about it. You don't have a date anyway, and you don't want to miss your prom."

"It's only the junior prom, Dad."

"Still. You'll regret not going. Trust me, okay? If not Liam, then think about someone else. Girls can ask guys to the prom, too, you know."

Joanie stood up abruptly. "That'll never happen," she said, stuffing her skates into their bag and heading for the house again. "I gotta go."

"Have fun!" her dad called after her.

It was too long a trip for her bike so this time Joanie's mom dropped her at the rink. Kate didn't seem to be there yet, so Joanie took her skates over to get them sharpened before she put them on. She'd skated a lot in middle school and even freshman year, but for some reason she and Zane just hadn't been in a long while. Too much homework, too many school commitments, something had always stopped them from going.

Joanie sat on the edge of one of the bleachers and laced

herself into her skates. They'd been new freshman year so they still fit pretty well, and as she stood up and found her balance, it started coming back to her. She tucked her skate bag underneath the bleacher seat, pulled her ear muffs on tighter and headed for the rink.

She set her blade guards on the bench by the entrance to the ring along with dozens of others and gingerly put one foot out on the ice. When that felt fairly stable, she added a second and pushed away from the wall. She glided along, putting down one foot, and then the other, starting to make her way around the ring. It was coming back easier than she thought it would and she picked up some speed, feeling the little rush of cold air on her cheeks and in her hair. She let her arms relax at her sides. She started up an easy rhythm, and the next thing she knew she was moving at a good clip around the ring.

It was so much fun it was hard not to grin like a fool, so she didn't bother to hide it. And she had no idea how long she'd been skating when Kate finally called her name.

"Hey! Joanie!" Kate shouted, waving.

"Come on!" Joanie waved back, gliding right by the spot where Kate was putting on her skates. She could hear Kate laughing as she zoomed away.

"Hey!" Kate stood at the edge of the ice a few minutes later, waiting for Joanie to come around again.

Joanie slowed way down, but didn't stop completely and she glided past Kate. "Come on."

"Wait! Hey, wait up!" Kate called, and Joanie realized she'd left Kate far behind. She stopped along the wall and waited for Kate, who seemed a great deal more uncertain on her skates than Joanie was.

"I'm so bad at this," Kate said, finally catching up. "I never really got the hang of it."

"You can't skate?"

"Not very well," Kate admitted.

"Well, then. I'll just have to help you." Joanie grinned and started skating backwards. "Just gently push off... one foot, then the other... good... see?"

Kate was biting her lip and looking down at her feet but she was moving. "Okay... yeah. This part I can do. Whoa!" She slipped and her arms started flailing and the next thing Joanie knew, Kate was flat on the ice.

"Oh, my God!" Kate was laughing but Joanie was worried anyway. "Are you okay?" She skated over and leaned over Kate, offering her a hand up.

"Fine, fine. I'm fine," Kate said, still laughing. "Sorry. I'm really bad at this. I am so going to bore you."

"No way. Come on."

Joanie helped Kate up and dusted the ice off her jacket, then she turned backward again and held out her hands. "Don't look down, stand up straight," she told Kate. Kate took her hands and started to move. But she was still looking down at her toes.

"Hey, up here. Look up here." Kate looked up and met Joanie's eyes and it was all Joanie could do not to get lost in their blueness again. "That's it," she told Kate, holding her hands tightly. "Slowly. Good!"

Kate looked a little uncertain, but she was starting to move more smoothly. "I can't believe you're skating backward."

Joanie shrugged. "I haven't skated in a long time. I thought I would have forgotten more, but I guess you just kind of remember this stuff."

"Cool." Kate gripped Joanie's hands tighter.

"Relax, it's okay. Just keep looking up, don't think too hard about your feet. Just glide, and glide... good.

Yeah." Joanie led Kate all the way around the ring like that, and then did it again. Joanie tried not to let herself think about what a great excuse this was to hold hands and stare into Kate's eyes.

By their third time around, Kate was doing well enough that, while Joanie was still skating backward, they weren't holding hands anymore. "Awesome!"

Kate was grinning. "Okay. Yeah. Not bad."

"You ready to try this on your own?" Joanie asked. "I'm going to get out of your way, okay?"

Kate nodded. "Okay. I got it. Slow, easy, eyes up, glide... yeah."

Joanie turned around and took off.

"Hey!"

"I'll catch up around the turn!" Joanie laughed, and dug into the ice.

She did, too, coming up on Kate's inside and taking her by the hand. She gave a light tug forcing Kate to pick up speed a little.

"Whoa, Joanie!"

"You're fine!"

Kate's grip tightened in hers. "I'm going to fall!"

"You're not!" Joanie laughed.

"I'm not?"

"You're fine."

"I am?"

"Kate, look at you."

Kate stopped biting her lip and looked around a little. They were moving together around the ring, not too fast, but easily and smoothly, and Joanie was only giving Kate light tugs to help keep her moving. She looked at Joanie and Joanie melted a little inside, again, like she always did when Kate smiled.

They managed to make it around the ring twice more without falling before Kate said she was tired.

"There's hot cider and stuff over there," Joanie said, pointing to a little kiosk that was selling food."

"Oh. Yes, please," Kate said, nodding.

Kate almost fell again when they stopped, but Joanie caught her, and they were still laughing about it as they slipped on their blade guards and headed for the kiosk.

Kate got hot chocolate and a brownie and Joanie got hot cider and an oatmeal raisin cookie, and they climbed up into the bleachers where they could get a good view of the skaters but still have a little privacy to talk.

"This is so good," Kate said, sipping her cocoa. "Warm. Yummy."

"I'm not really a chocolate fan," Joanie said. "I know that's weird. Zane tells me that all the time. He says I'm a freak."

Kate gasped dramatically. "You *are* a freak. How can you not like chocolate?"

"I don't know," Joanie shrugged, "I just don't."

Kate laughed. "I don't know if I can date you anymore."

"I've been dumped over worse things than chocolate," Joanie said with a snort.

"Like what?"

"Huh?"

"What else have you been dumped over?"

"Oh. Well." Joanie shrugged. She hadn't meant to get into a discussion about dating again. "I kind of dated this other girl once. We'd watch movies and hang out a lot and we'd give each other little notes and presents and stuff."

"Sounds nice. Why did she dump you?"

"Oh, she said she wasn't sure she, you know. She wasn't ready, I guess and... she ended up asking a guy out."

Kate nodded. "Been there. That sucks."

Joanie shrugged. "It hurt a little I guess, but it wasn't that big a deal. I just... haven't really dated anyone since."

"Really? No one?"

Joanie nodded.

"Well this is definitely a date," Kate told her, scooting an inch or two closer.

Joanie felt herself blush. "I was hoping it was."

"And I'm not going to dump you for a guy." Kate took a huge bite of her brownie and grinned as she chewed it.

"Oh, ho! So you might dump me for another girl?"

"How could I dump you? You just saw me fall on my ass. You could hold that over me for the rest of my life!"

"Blackmail!"

"Exactly!"

They both laughed pretty hard.

"Well." Joanie looked up to see Zane standing over them. "Joanie, you didn't tell me you guys would be here."

"Hey, Zane." It was true, she hadn't told Zane. She hadn't wanted to because this was a date, and Zane might have gotten upset about it. But not asking her best friend to go skating, well, he was definitely going to be upset now. Joanie cringed a little inside but tried not to look a guilty as she felt.

"Hi, Zane!" Kate stood up and gave him a kiss on the cheek. Joanie saw him blush and wondered if Kate had noticed, too.

"Uh. Hi, Kate. So... you guys are skating?"

Kate nodded. "That's what people do at a skating rink. Although I'm not sure you could call what I was doing, 'skating'."

"What?" Joanie jumped in without thinking. "You did great! You're not super fast, but you were skating just fine."

"She taught me," Kate said, patting Joanie's knee. "She's good."

"I taught *her*," Zane told Kate and then looked at Joanie. "Didn't I?"

Joanie nodded. "Yep... you did." Oh, God, the guilty feeling wasn't going away.

"Well, I guess I should leave you two alone, huh?"

"Zane," Joanie grabbed his coat sleeve. "You can hang out if..."

"No, no," Zane protested. "Don't let me interrupt. You ladies have a nice evening." Zane stepped over one of the bleacher seats and hobbled in his skate guards back down to the rink.

"Crap." Joanie sighed and sat down on the bleachers again. "Shit."

"Is he mad?"

"I think he might be. I didn't tell him we were... he didn't know we were going to be here, and he is my best friend, so."

"Oh, Joanie, I didn't mean to do that."

"I know. You didn't do anything, Kate. He's just not... used to things working out this way, you know?"

"Oh. Yeah. You mean when you both like someone? A girl?" Kate seemed to get it, she was pretty understanding about stuff. And she seemed to like Zane, too, as a friend anyway. Joanie was glad she didn't have to go into a long explanation.

"Yeah. He's so handsome," Joanie said with a sigh. "He always gets the girls."

It had happened to Joanie plenty of times. She and Zane would talk about a girl, Joanie would like her, too, but Zane was used to being the one the girl was actually interested in. Joanie just expected things to work out that way, and at this point, so did Zane. This thing with Kate was completely unexpected, and Joanie didn't have any idea how to handle it with her best friend, especially knowing that Zane really had a crush on Kate. She'd thought keeping it low-key and quiet was the best thing at first, but apparently, she'd made the wrong choice. Joanie felt terrible about that.

Kate looked after Zane and Joanie followed her gaze. Zane was on the ice now and skating fast rings around the outside, passing people left and right. He had on his hockey skates, the black ones that Joanie had always admired. Joanie kept hoping she'd outgrow her figure skates so she'd have a reason to ask for new ones, but her feet hadn't gotten any bigger since freshman year.

Kate looked back at Joanie. "He is handsome, it's true. And he is a good skater, too. But he didn't get the girl this time, Joanie. That's just something he's going to have to live with. You're the one I'm interested in. Can you handle that?"

Joanie's eyes grew wide and she blinked stupidly at Kate for a moment. "Yeah. Yeah, I can handle it. I just..."

Kate smiled and leaned in close, kissing Joanie lightly on the lips. Joanie's got a little lightheaded at first but then that stupid panic set in. Had anyone seen? She looked around Kate toward the ice.

Kate laughed. "Sure you can handle it?"

"Kate, you know I'm not out."

"And you know I am. Sooner or later people are going to figure things out, Joanie."

Joanie looked back at Kate and nodded. "Yeah, I know."

Kate's eyes softened a bit and she smiled. "Want to see me fall on my ass again?" She took Joanie by the hand. "Come on."

Joanie tried to approach Zane on the ice but he skated away and she lost track of him for the rest of the night. She looked for him again when they came off the ice but she couldn't find him and she figured he'd gone home.

"My mom'll be here soon," Kate said as they took their skates off and put on their shoes.

"Yeah, my dad, too."

Kate looked around and then motioned for Joanie to follow her. "Come here."

"What is it?" Joanie hopped up and hurried to follow.

Kate led her through the rink and out a side door. She looked in both directions and then took Joanie's hand and tugged her around the corner. "Can I kiss you now?"

"Oh." Joanie felt her heart start to pound in her chest. "Uh. Kate... here?"

"There's no one around."

To be honest, she wanted to kiss Kate, too. Joanie looked left and right and then looked back at Kate. She didn't trust herself to speak so she just nodded.

Kate smiled and leaned forward, and Joanie met her halfway. Their lips touched, Kate's fingers rested on Joanie's shoulder and Joanie felt like everything was spinning. She really didn't know how long they kissed – longer than the peck in the bleachers for sure. When Kate pulled away Joanie lost her balance and reached out and grabbed Kate's arm.

Kate caught her, and she was smiling, but she didn't say anything. They just looked at each other for a long time, until Joanie's mind cleared and she could smile back.

"Good?" Kate asked.

Joanie nodded. Way good. Much better than whatever she and Zane did in his living room, which now she couldn't even call kissing. That was... stupid. What she and Kate just did, the way it made Joanie feel, that was a real kiss.

And just like in eighth grade when she had to tell Zane her discovery, she had an urge to rush out and find him to tell him all about that kiss.

But she this time didn't.

Joanie and Kate waited for their parents together, sitting on a bench outside the rink with a good foot of space between them. Joanie's fingers seemed to itch. She wanted to hold Kate's hand so badly but she just couldn't. Not yet. Every so often she'd look over at Kate and Kate would smile at her, but neither of them really said anything.

Joanie's dad arrived first. Kate stood up with her and hugged her goodbye. "You okay?"

"Yeah," Joanie smiled at her. "Good. Great."

"Call me tomorrow?"

Joanie nodded. "Promise."

Kate waved as Joanie's dad pulled away.

"Did you have fun?" her dad asked, halfway home.

"Yeah."

"Tired?" He must have noticed how quiet she was.

Joanie just nodded. "Yeah."

But she wasn't actually tired. She was thinking. She had a lot to think about. At home, alone in her room, she got out her journal and chewed on her pen cap. There was so much to sort out now. She *had* to talk to Zane, she just had to. She had to figure out what to tell her parents, too. Did she want her friends at school to know? Would people treat her differently once they knew? Would her dad be mad?

Joanie lay back in her pillows and stared at the ceiling, trying not to be afraid, but she was. It was so much to think about all at once.

She liked Kate. She'd always told herself that she would tell her parents when they needed to know and she'd kissed Kate now. They were probably officially girlfriends, although Kate hadn't used that word yet. Did that mean her parents needed to know? What words should she use? Should she tell them about Kate right away, too, or wait? Should she tell them both at the same time? Should she tell her sister?

It was overwhelming, with all the questions she was trying to answer at once, and at some point Joanie fell asleep, still thinking about it.

CHAPTER TWELVE

When Joanie woke up the next morning she still didn't have any answers and she hadn't written a word in her journal, either. Weirder than that, she didn't even have a single sketch or anything to show for all the time she'd spent thinking. It worried her a little that things had become so confusing that she couldn't even get her thoughts down on paper.

It was sunny and beautiful outside though, one of the first real spring days they'd had so far, and Joanie thought maybe some air might help. She stuffed her journal in her backpack, swallowed down a quick breakfast and hurried out the door.

She stopped on the corner and pulled out her cell phone to send Zane a text.

Going to visit the Truherns, gonna draw, write. Hope to see you there. Want to talk.

The graveyard was quiet as usual, and Joanie found a seat in the sunshine leaning up against Alice's gravestone. She pulled out her journal and started to write.

Tell Mom first? No. Tell Dad first. Let Dad tell Mom. Except that's kind of chicken-shit of me. Tell Mom and Dad together.

After the prom?

The prom. Joanie really did want to go. She liked dancing, and she wanted to see Zane in a tux. Maybe she would ask Zane after all. Or just go with the guy her dad was talking about. At least she'd have a date.

She started to draw, first a little sketch of herself in a prom dress. What would she wear? Honestly, she had no idea. Something in a subtle, neutral color no doubt, maybe two pieces, like a top with spaghetti straps and a long skirt. Her mother's pearls. Chunky heels, because she was a disaster waiting to happen in spiky-heeled dress shoes.

Next to herself she drew Zane in a tux. She made him a little geeky, his pant legs a little too short, his hair combed over and practically glued down to look formal and conservative. Spats on his shoes. An over-large crooked bowtie.

On her other side, she drew Kate. Kate's hair flowed out behind her, her dress was long and classically feminine. A basic black, maybe. Strapless. Long to the ground with a skirt that would swish around her ankles when she danced. Strappy sandals. Sparkly necklace and earrings. Oh, Kate would look like a movie star, tall and beautiful like Nicole Kidman or something. At least in Joanie's mind.

She sketched the scene, and added in a tall stranger in the background that was meant to be that Liam guy that her dad had mentioned. She made him bulkier than Zane, broader in the shoulders and his tux wasn't as geeky. But even looking at the scene in her familiar cartoon style didn't make her feel better about it.

It was almost noon when Joanie sent Zane another text.

Come on, Zane. We need to talk. I'm sorry.

When she was done with that one, she sent one to Kate.

Had fun last night. Have work to do. Will call later.

She got an answer back from Kate almost immediately.

me 2. big bruise on my butt. ouch. :D

Joanie laughed and wrote Kate's name a million times over in her journal.

When Joanie's stomach started to growl she packed up her things. She checked her phone one more time, but there was nothing from Zane.

Kate likes girls..., she sent, in one final attempt to get his attention, and then she stuffed her phone into her pocket.

Zane never wrote her back. Joanie should have known this was going to be a bad day.

When she got home, she scrounged in the fridge for a late lunch, finding some leftover lasagna, which she heated up in the microwave.

"Don't eat too much," her mom said, coming into the kitchen. "You'll spoil your dinner."

Joanie rolled her eyes. "I'm hungry, Mom, geez."

"We're going to your grandmother's tomorrow, don't forget."

"We are?"

"I told you two days ago, Joanie."

"Do I have to go?"

"Don't start with me, Joanie. It's her birthday and you're going."

Joanie sat down at the table to eat. "Fine."

"Hey, Joanie." Her dad came in and gave her a pat on the shoulder. "Save some for me?"

"There's a ton."

"I don't know why I bother to make dinner when all anyone does in this house is eat all day."

"I'm hungry!" Joanie and her dad said at the same time. They both laughed, and Joanie's mother just shook her head.

Her dad sat down at the table with her. "So did you think about Liam?"

"Dad..."

"Who's Liam?" Joanie's mom asked.

"Dad." Joanie gestured to her mom. "Now look what you did!"

"Liam Andrews," her dad answered simply.

"Oh, Rick and Sherri's son?"

"That's the one."

"Oh, Joanie, did he ask you to the prom?"

"No, Mom!" Joanie looked at her dad.

"I suggested that since Liam was looking for a date, Joanie might want to go with him."

"Liam's a handsome boy, Joanie. Why not?"

Joanie looked between them. "I don't even know him."

"His parents are nice people, Joanie."

"So? Maybe he's a jerk!" Joanie tossed her fork into her plate, suddenly not hungry anymore. "Will you guys *please* knock it off?"

"What?" Joanie's mother looked genuinely clueless, and she probably was.

"Nagging me about the prom? Trying to set me up with people? Cut it out."

"But Joanie, it's only two weeks away. You need a dress and we'll have to get it altered… he'll need to order flowers. You can't wait until last minute."

Joanie's dad looked across the table at her. "Do you want to go, Joanie?"

She bit her lip and looked at her dad for a minute. "Yeah. I do want to go but I don't know if…"

"Do you think you'll find another date before then?"

Joanie sighed. "I don't know." Kate came to mind, but that was a whole other set of things to think about and Joanie was already confused enough. "No. Probably not."

"I'll ask about Liam, okay? At least you can go and dance and have a good time."

"Fine, Dad. Ask Liam. I don't care anymore." Joanie got up from the table and went to her room.

It was time to stop thinking about everything and make some decisions.

CHAPTER THIRTEEN

Joanie didn't text Zane again. She didn't call Kate either, although she wanted to. She just didn't know what to say. After her conversation about the prom with her parents she just wasn't feeling very confident in her ability to tell anybody anything, least of all her parents. If she needed an excuse she'd just say she went to her grandmother's and forgot her phone.

But Monday morning came whether she was ready for it or not, and that meant she had to go to the bus stop. It meant Zane had to go, too, so Joanie got up early to make sure they had time to talk.

"Oh, my God, you're on time. Are you sick?" Liz said, poking Joanie in the arm as she walked by.

"Shut up." Joanie grabbed a banana and a granola bar and headed for the door.

"Coat!"

"Mom, it's warm out." Joanie shook her head as she headed for the door.

"It's not as warm as you think!" her mom's voice

followed her out the door.

The bus stop was deserted, with no sign of Zane. Joanie dumped her backpack on the ground and stood next to it as she pulled out her phone to send him a text.

Where are you?

The answer came back quickly.

Right behind you.

Joanie turned around to find Zane standing two feet away. "Jesus, you snuck up on me."

"You're early. Did someone die?"

"You know, I'm not late every day," Joanie protested.

"Yeah, you are." Zane stuffed his phone in his pocket and then his hands.

"I'm sorry about the other night. I should have told you we were going."

"Would have been nice. I mean, it looked like you didn't want me to be there."

"It wasn't that. I mean, it was sort of but not like you think. I just…"

"She seriously likes girls?"

"Yeah, she does."

"So, that was a *date*?" Zane asked.

Joanie nodded. "It was. A real date." She tried not to smile, but she couldn't help it.

Zane nodded slowly. "And that's why you didn't invite me."

"Yeah. And plus I was kind of afraid you'd be mad that she asked me out."

"I'm not mad."

Joanie squinted at him. "Seriously?"

"I mean, I was mad. I really was. But if Kate likes girls… well, it's not like she'd have dated me anyway."

"No." Joanie shook her head. "She's totally out. Her

parents know and everything."

"Well, that sucks." Zane sighed.

"For you."

Zane laughed and Joanie started to feel better about everything. "Yeah, for me. It's awesome for you, though Joanie."

"You're okay with it, then?"

"Sure. I'll get over being dumped for a girl eventually." He grinned.

"So," Joanie stepped closer and spoke more quietly, even though she and Zane were the only two at the bus stop. "Guess what?"

"What?"

"She… kissed me."

Zane's eyes grew wide. "No way!"

"Uh-huh."

"Wow. Was it good? I mean, she seems so…"

"It was good. I got all goofy and blushed and felt lightheaded and the whole thing."

"Geez, Joanie. I think I'm jealous." Zane tried to sound like he was joking, but Joanie knew that part of him wasn't. He seemed like he'd be okay, though. They both stepped back from the curb as the bus arrived. "So… are you going to tell your parents now?"

Joanie waited to answer that question until they were on the bus. "I don't know. Not yet."

"Why not?"

"The whole *prom* thing."

"Oh. Right. What are you going to do?"

"They're setting me up with some guy. Liam Andrews?"

"The football player?"

"He plays *football*?"

"Yep."

Joanie sighed. "God, we're not going to have anything to talk about, are we?"

"You're actually going to go with him?"

"Why, are you jealous again?" Joanie grinned, poking Zane in the thigh.

Zane glanced at her sidelong and then looked out the window. "No, I... Well, I was trying to figure out how to tell you anyway so, I... asked Samantha."

Joanie sat up. "Whoa, what? Who?"

"You heard me."

"Samantha Lee?"

"Joanie, don't be a jerk."

Joanie was more than a little surprised. "But you guys broke up months ago."

"Yeah, we did."

"And?"

"Well? She didn't have a date, I didn't have a date; we got to talking..."

Joanie actually liked Samantha. She'd been the only girlfriend Zane had ever had that Joanie really liked. She never really understood why they broke up. They'd had some stupid argument and the next thing she knew Samantha wasn't speaking to him and he wasn't talking about her anymore. Joanie had tried to ask what was up a couple of times, but Zane always changed the subject. He'd seemed really upset.

Joanie had a million questions about why they were talking all of a sudden, when they saw each other last, whether they were getting back together, but "Cool," was all Joanie said. For now.

"Yeah." Zane looked at her and smiled and Joanie couldn't help but smile back.

"So, we're good then?" Joanie asked.

"Yeah. We're good. Sorry if I was kind of an ass."

"Sorry I didn't tell you the truth."

"It's cool," Zane said. "But I'm still jealous." He grinned at her as the bus parked in front of the school and got up. "Seen her since?"

"No."

"Oh, this is going to be a fun day," Zane teased.

"Zane!"

"Bye!" Zane practically ran off the bus.

CHAPTER FOURTEEN

Thursday couldn't have come soon enough. Sure, Joanie wanted her license but that wasn't the reason she was so impatient to see Gary, her driving instructor, again. It would be nice to just hang out with someone that knew who she was and didn't make a big deal out of it.

"Hey," Gary said as he got out of the driver's side and moved around the car to get into the passenger's seat. "How goes?"

"Okay." Joanie shrugged as she got behind the wheel.

"We're hitting the highway today."

"We are?"

"Yep. Has your dad taken you out to I-95 yet?"

"Nope. Never even mentioned it."

"Well, today you drive fifty-five, my friend. Buckle up." Joanie put on her seatbelt and started the car. Gary patted her on the shoulder. "Don't be nervous."

"Okay."

Gary laughed. "You'll be fine."

"If you say so."

"Seriously."

Joanie drove out of the school and made a left, heading down Ridge Road toward the highway. They didn't talk much, apart from Gary giving her directions, until they hit the onramp to I-95.

"Okay, signal so they know you're coming over and get in the middle lane."

"The middle?"

"Yes. It's the safest, you have the most options."

"Can't I poke along in the slow lane?"

"No. Don't be chicken. Move over."

Chicken pretty much described everything about her life these days. Joanie signaled, checked her mirrors, looked over her shoulder, checked her mirrors again. "I can go now?"

"Yep. Go on."

Joanie shifted into the middle lane. It was easier than she'd expected it to be. "Okay."

"See? Not so bad. How fast are you going?"

"I'm going..." Joanie glanced at the speedometer. "Oh, wow."

"Fifty-five?"

"Yeah, how did that happen?"

"Congratulations, you're highway driving." Gary grinned and Joanie grinned back.

"Cool."

They drove for about half an hour, changing lanes and taking on and off ramps, driving up and down the same stretch of highway until Joanie felt like she had the hang of it.

"Don't speed, use your signals and keep your eyes open."

"You got it."

"Great. Head back into town."

"How do I get there?"

"Any way you want."

"...oh."

"Think about it, you know the way."

Joanie took the next exit, and then took a series of roads she knew would get her back into town. Somerset to Drysner, Drysner to Lilac, Lilac to Route 40 to Main Street. Gary read a magazine the whole way.

Or at least he pretended to.

"We're here," Joanie said to get his attention.

"Yeah? Thank God. You took the longest route ever. I thought we'd never get here."

"Shut up."

Gary laughed. "Hey, it's your gas money; I don't care how you get where you're going. Any questions?"

Joanie drove down Main, headed into the center of town. "Yeah. My dad set me up with some guy for the prom. What do I do?"

"Put on your left blinker and turn up here."

Joanie sighed. "Sorry. It's okay if you don't want to answer that question."

"Pull into that parking lot and park the car."

Joanie parked, pulling the nose in carefully.

"Nice job."

"Thank you."

"So what's this, now? You're going to the prom with some guy you don't know?"

"Yes."

"Hm. Well. You haven't told them about Kate, I guess."

"Right."

"Do you want to go to the prom?"

"Yeah, I do."

"Well, then go and have fun. Maybe this guy will be nice. Some guys are, you know."

Joanie snorted. "Yeah, yeah. My best friend is a guy."

"See? We're not all pigs."

"I didn't say he wasn't a pig." Joanie grinned and Gary laughed.

"So, tell me the truth, Joanie. And you can, because I'm only your driving instructor. You're going to see a whole six hours of me – three of which are already over – and then you never have to see me again. Right? So tell me. You know for sure that you're gay?"

Joanie looked at her hands for a while, the looked at Gary. "Yeah. For sure."

"And you can't tell your parents?"

"I don't know. I should."

"Is Kate out?"

"Yeah, she is."

"And you're dating her?"

"Yep."

"Well, it sounds to me like you have some thinking to do."

"Yeah, I know. I will. I'll figure it out."

"I know you will."

"Is the lesson over?"

Gary snorted. "That one is. This one isn't. Back out to Main Street, please."

Joanie rolled her eyes.

CHAPTER FIFTEEN

On my way.

Joanie read the text message and smiled. The only thing cooler than visiting the Truherns during the day was visiting them at night. It was almost dusk now and Joanie leaned against Owen's grave marker, eyes toward the winding, hilly road that led toward the street and the church. Sure enough, she spotted a figure coming up over the small rise.

She waved, and Kate waved back, picking up her pace. "Creepy!" Kate called out as she got closer.

"It's not creepy. We're safe with the Truherns; they're old friends."

"If you say so." Kate stepped right up to Joanie and kissed her on the cheek. "Thanks for inviting me."

Joanie took her hand. "Thank you for coming."

"So why here?"

"Because it's walking distance from home."

"Okay."

"And it's... kind of private."

Kate smiled. "Is Zane going to show up again?"

"No. He knows I'm meeting you here; I asked him if it was okay."

"You asked if it was okay for us to meet here? Why do you need his permission?"

"Because this is our place. His and mine. We've spent years hanging out here after school talking and arguing and crying and dreaming up all kinds of things. Hours and hours. I didn't want to show it to you unless he said it was okay."

Kate nodded. "Yeah, okay. I see what you mean then." She leaned on Alex's grave stone and smiled. "So he was cool with it I guess?"

"He was. He says hello, too."

Kate pushed off the headstone and wandered a bit, squinting to read the markers in the fading light. "Um, Joanie?"

"Yeah?"

"Didn't you just tell me you knew these people?"

"Well, yeah, sort of."

"They died over a hundred years ago."

Joanie laughed. "I'm a ghost. You didn't know?"

Kate glanced at her. "Quit it; you're creeping me out."

Joanie snorted. "I meant that we've made up stories about all of them. How they lived, who they married, what they did for a living... just to entertain ourselves. We don't really *know* them."

"O... kay," Kate said skeptically. "So who was this guy? Daniel Truhern?"

"He was a librarian. Died a bachelor. His one true love was married off by her parents to a rich and influential man she didn't love and they both died a year later on the same day of broken hearts."

"Ha!" Kate laughed. "And Alex?"

"He died robbing a bank."

"Cool."

"Well, cool if you like dying at twenty-six years old."

"Wow. Twenty-six?"

Joanie nodded.

"So what if you found my gravestone? What stories would you make up about me?"

"That depends on how long you lived."

Kate crossed her arms. "Okay. Let's say I lived to be eighty."

"Oh, nice. My grandmother just turned eighty. She's still a firecracker. I think you would be, too."

"Yeah?"

"Yeah. A little slow moving, but mentally sharp as a tack. Let's see. Kate Dalton. Died at age eighty of... a heart attack, while... waterskiing."

"Waterskiing? Are you nuts?"

"Hush. Who's making things up here?"

Kate laughed. "Go on, then."

"Okay, so..." Joanie sat on the Truhern family marker. It was wide and flat on top and she pulled herself up to perch on it and watch Kate. "Kate was best known for her... gold medal in the Geriatric Olympics in figure skating. Her innovative use of a walker on the ice made her a granny ahead of her time."

"Oh, shut up."

"What? I'm missing something?"

"Yeah. Did I graduate from college?"

"Sure. With a degree in chemistry."

"As if." Kate snorted and Joanie laughed. "Did I ever find love?"

Joanie smiled. "Yeah. You married your high school sweetheart, of course."

"No kidding?" Kate stepped closer, leaning on the stone where Joanie was sitting. "Did it last?"

"Of course."

Kate leaned forward and Joanie didn't hesitate, meeting her halfway and returning her kiss. Kate smelled sweet, like cherries or strawberries, and Joanie stroked a hand down her long, soft hair. When they pulled away, Kate stared at her.

"You think this is love?" she asked after a while.

"I don't know." Joanie answered honestly. "Maybe? Have you ever been in love?"

"No."

"Me neither."

"But this feels like it."

Joanie nodded. "It feels like it to me, too."

"Okay, then it must be." Kate slipped her hand into Joanie's. "That okay?"

"Yeah, it's good." Joanie smiled. "It's perfect."

"So, uh. Any kids?"

Joanie blinked. "Kids?"

"In my fake future."

"Oh! Uh. Yes. Two. A boy and a girl."

"Nice."

"The boy was named Zane after a famous nuclear scientist."

Kate made a face. "Yuck. Is that what he wants to do?"

"Something like that, I don't know. Scientist, lab research, something."

"God, he is such a geek."

"He really is." Joanie grinned. "But he's a nice guy. A

real guy, you know? Genuine."

Kate nodded. "Seems like."

"So yeah, a boy named Zane and a girl named... Elizabeth, after your high school sweetheart's sister who never married because she was such a pain in the ass."

They both laughed.

"So, I have another question."

Joanie looked at Kate. "Yes?"

"Did my high school sweetheart ever come out to her parents or did people think we were roommates for sixty years?"

"Ha ha ha." Joanie slid off the stone and walked a few steps away.

"Yeah, that's funny, huh?"

Joanie sighed. "Come on, Kate, that's not fair." It was dark now and it was hard to see Kate's face even from a few feet away. She was silhouetted against one of the lamps that lit the path back to the street.

"Look, it's not that I want to pressure you, Joanie, really. It's just... look. You're a great person, and I really do think we have something amazing starting to happen here. But I'm not going to go back into hiding, you know? I did the coming out thing already and I'm ready to get on with being me. I can handle it for a little while, but I'd really like to date someone that's... ready to be themselves, too."

Joanie stared at Kate. "Wait. Are you saying that you won't date me if I don't come out?"

"No. Joanie, I'm not saying that. It's just..." Kate went silent for a minute and then started again. "Well, maybe I am a little. I mean, you don't have to come out tomorrow, Joanie, but you have to promise you're going to. Pretty soon, you know?"

"What's pretty soon? A week? A month? I don't know when I'm going to be ready, Kate."

Kate sighed and walked toward Joanie. "Okay, that's... that's okay, Joanie. You have to do these things when you're ready, I know that. It's no good if you're not there yet. Just think about it. Hopefully it won't be too long and I'll be able to wait, you know?" She kissed Joanie quickly on the cheek.

Joanie searched Kate's eyes feeling tears coming. "What if I can't... decide not to tell them?"

Kate shrugged. "I don't know. I guess... I just hope you will. Just think about it, please?" Kate gave Joanie's hand a squeeze.

The last thing Joanie wanted to do right now was cry in front of Kate. "I gotta go."

"Joanie..."

"I'll see you later, Kate."

"Call me, Joanie? Okay?"

Joanie moved past Kate quickly, hurrying to where her bicycle was leaning against a tree, and barely made it out of the graveyard before the tears began to fall.

Chapter Sixteen

Joanie and her mom spent all day Saturday looking for a prom dress. Her mom wanted her to be pretty and conservative, but Joanie wanted something a little more... fun. They finally found a two piece with spaghetti straps, which was what Joanie wanted, in a kind of gold-ish brown color. Her mother called it "bronze". Much better than the pinks and purples that her mom kept picking out for her to try on. The skirt was more what her mother had wanted, though, long to the floor and A-line. It was a compromise that Joanie could live with.

The shoes were another battle entirely. Joanie wanted solid heels that she could dance in and not fall on her face or end up in pain by the end of the night, but her mom kept showing her spiked, delicate-looking things that barely held your foot in.

"Mom, do you want me to break my neck?"

"Joanie..."

"MOM."

In the end Joanie ended up with a cheaper pair of wide

heels that she felt comfortable in and her mom didn't argue because she liked the price tag.

Good, that's done, Joanie thought. *Thank God.*

"Now, Joanie, honey, can we talk about your hair?"

Joanie did her best not to glare at her mother. Naturally, she would bring up something controversial like Joanie's hair when Joanie was a prisoner in a moving car and couldn't walk away. "Can we talk about your hair" was the way her mother started the conversation every time she wanted to tell Joanie how much she disliked the slightly disheveled look Joanie favored.

"You want to look pretty, sweetheart, not like you just got out of bed."

"Do you have any idea how long I style my hair to get the 'just got out of bed' look, Mom?"

"I hate to think." Joanie's mom snorted.

"Why does it matter to you? You're not going to the prom, I am."

"Boys like girls to look beautiful."

"Zane says I'm beautiful."

"Joanie, honey, Zane doesn't count."

Joanie shook her head.

"I'm not saying you have to cut it, Joanie, just, comb it. Maybe give it a nice side part and sweep your bangs over? I can help you with it if you want."

"We'll see." That seemed better than an outright no.

"I'll see if I can find some pictures of what I am taking about."

"You do that."

"Joanie, why does everything have to be a battle with you these days? You haven't seemed happy in weeks. Hiding up in your room, even Liz thinks you've been unfriendly."

"Liz? Is everyone in the family talking about me now?"

"We're just worried about you, honey."

"Well, don't worry. I'm fine." *Just leave me alone*, she thought.

"You're obviously not fine, Joanie."

"It's none of your business. Okay?"

Joanie's mom looked at her. "All right, but maybe your father..."

"Well at least he doesn't nag me all the time."

"Joanie!"

Joanie got out of the car and ran into the house.

"Hey! How did it...?" her dad started to ask as she ran past him and up the stairs.

She heard him asking her mom what happened just before she slammed her bedroom door.

Joanie's mom was right, she was unhappy. She had gone from taking about love with Kate to having a broken heart in one conversation.

She paced around her room not knowing what to do with herself. She turned on the radio but that didn't distract her. She tried to do some homework but she couldn't concentrate on it, either. She flipped through her journal but couldn't really make herself read it.

Finally she gave up and picked up the phone.

"I knew you were going to call me, how did dress shopping go?"

"It sucked."

"Did you find a dress?"

"Yes. It's okay, I guess."

"Okay..."

"Kate broke up with me." There was a long silence on the other end of the line. "Zane?"

"Yes?"

"Did you hear me?"

"Yes, I just couldn't decide if you'd rather hear 'what a bitch', or 'I'm so sorry.'"

"She's not a bitch."

"Okay then, I'm really sorry," Zane said, sounding sincere. "She seriously broke up with you? I don't get it."

"Well, maybe she didn't break up with me exactly. But she doesn't want to date me if I don't come out."

"So come out."

"Zane!"

"What?"

"It's not that simple!"

"Joanie..."

"I don't get how she can do this to me!" Joanie couldn't help it; she burst into tears. She really didn't know how long she cried, but Zane just hung on, quietly.

"Do you want me to come over?"

"No, no. It's okay."

"Look, Joanie?" Zane asked quietly. "Are you sure she broke up with you?"

"No. I guess not. I'm not sure about anything." Joanie blew her nose.

"Nice."

"Shut up, jerk."

"Remember Brooke?"

"You mean the last girl who dumped me? Thanks, Zane!"

"Wait, wait, listen. She dumped you for a guy because she wasn't ready to admit she was gay, remember?"

"That was different; she didn't want to believe it herself."

"Is it? I mean, she wasn't ready to come out to herself… you aren't ready to come out to your parents…"

Joanie went quiet and swiped at her eyes.

"It's the same thing. Sort of."

Joanie nodded, realizing that Zane was right. Kate wanted to hold hands in public. She wanted a girlfriend that she could date for real, not in cemeteries and behind ice rinks where no one was looking. Joanie was the one who was scared, now, just like Brooke had been. She was the one who wasn't ready to be herself, the one who wasn't in the same mental place as Kate. This time Kate was the one who was asking for more.

And Joanie was out buying a dress for a prom she was going to with a guy she didn't even know.

"Oh, Zane."

"Am I still a jerk?"

"Yes, but you're forgiven." Joanie sniffled and then blew her nose again.

"Nice."

"Shut up, jerk."

"Are you okay?"

"Yeah. I think so. I will be. I just… need to tell my parents. Thanks, Zane."

"I still think you should tell Liz and let her blab," Zane joked. Well, he had better have been joking.

"Ha ha ha. Goodnight."

"Goodnight, Joanie."

CHAPTER SEVENTEEN

Two more hours of lessons and that was all. Her plan was to get in the car, drive, and come home, saying as little as possible about her predicament because somehow she knew what Gary would tell her. Why she felt as if she had more responsibility to her Driver's Ed instructor than to her family or herself, she'd never know.

They drove to the high school parking lot where Gary got out and set up orange traffic cones. "Parallel paaaaaarkiiiiiing!" he sang, getting back in the car.

"Crap."

"It's required, Joanie," Gary said, pulling a pair of drumsticks out of the glove compartment. "So. Pull up alongside that cone."

Joanie stared at the drumsticks for a second. "Okay..." She looked away from his drumsticks and did as she was told.

"Great. Now put it in reverse and then turn the wheel the direction you want the back end to go."

"Are you... that feels wrong."

"Would I steer you wrong?" Gary grinned.

"Ugh." More driving jokes. "That one sucked."

"Trust me, I've been doing this a long time."

Joanie did as he said and maneuvered the back end into the parking space. It worked.

"Oh, cool."

"Good, now put it in drive and turn the wheel in the direction you want the front end to go."

Joanie bit her lip and tried to pull the front end into the parking space, neatly running over the cone in front. "Oops."

Gary got out of the car, fixed the cone and got back in again. "Congratulations! You just dented the back end of the very sleek and expensive car in front of you and sent your parents' insurance rates through the roof. Back up, pull up alongside the cone, try again." He leaned forward and put on a Nickelback CD, then sat back in his seat and started to drum on the dashboard.

"What... what are you doing?" Joanie shouted over the music.

"What?"

She rolled her eyes and shouted louder, "What. Are. You. Doing?"

Gary grinned at her and shrugged. "Practicing!"

"What if I need help?"

"Trust me, I can't help you. You just have to keep trying until you get it."

Joanie sighed and pulled out of the parking space to try again. She hit the curb on the next try, she ran over a different cone after that, but eventually something clicked and she got the car into the spot on the fourth try. Okay, yes, it was two feet from the curb, but she didn't hit anything or run anything over. Twenty minutes and five or six Nickelback songs later, she pulled the car into the parking spot three times in a row. Slowly, yes, but neatly. And thank God, because if she had to listen to "Figured You Out" one more time, she was going to lose her mind.

Gary leaned forward and shut the radio off. "Nice work."

"I thought you weren't paying attention."

"Yeah, I lied." He winked at Joanie. "And you did pretty good, too. Most people stop and yell at me to turn the music down long before they get it."

"Ha! As if you'd have turned it down even if I had yelled at you," Joanie said with a snort. "No point in asking."

"You're right! But I *was* paying attention and if you hadn't been making progress on your own I would have said something. The thing about parallel parking is that it's not as hard as everyone thinks it is. You just have to understand how the car moves. I can't teach that part."

"Dad's gonna be impressed."

"And... what's her name? Kate?"

Joanie shrugged, not answering. "Where to now?"

Gary looked at her for a moment and then got out of the car to retrieve the cones. When he got back to the passenger seat he put his drumsticks the glove compartment. "We have an hour. What do you feel like you need? More highway? Tight turns in town?"

"Let's do town," Joanie suggested.

"Town it is. You're behind the wheel."

Joanie sighed and pulled out of the parking lot. "If only every decision was that easy."

Gary looked at her again.

"Don't look at me like that; you know what I'm talking about."

"Kate?"

"She likes me. But I'm not out."

"And... you don't want to come out?"

"I do. I do want to. I think." Joanie bit her lip and turned right on Forrest.

"Awesome."

"No. Not awesome."

"Not awesome?"

"No. I have to figure out how first of all, and second of all, I just let my mother buy me a dress for the prom."

"And you're going with...?"

Joanie came to a full and complete stop at a stop sign before answering. "My parents set me up."

"Ah. With a guy."

"Well, of course."

"Does Kate know that?" Gary pointed. "Hang a left."

Joanie hesitated. "No. She doesn't know that."

"Ohh. I see. Not awesome."

"Not at all." Joanie turned left and headed down Main Street.

"Well, I don't know anything about relationships because I'm just a driving instructor, but I do know about driving. And when you drive, you don't get where you want to go sitting around in neutral."

Joanie glanced over at him. "Do you have *any* idea how hokey that sounds?"

"Yep," Gary nodded. "Hokey, but true."

"Totally hokey," Joanie said, nodding back. "But true."

The last hour of her driving lessons went by quickly.

The drove the length of Main Street, then drove out to the high school, and the next thing she knew, she was home.

"Well?" Joanie said, somehow unwilling to get out of the car.

"Well, I'm passing you. You can take your test as early as your birthday," Gary told her. "Congratulations."

"Thanks." Joanie took the paperwork from him.

"You're ready."

"Are you sure?"

"Yep, you are. It'll feel a little weird at first, like the day your dad took the training wheels off your bicycle, you know? Wobbly. Just take it slow and keep practicing."

Joanie nodded to him as she got out of the car. Gary hopped out, too and got in on the driver's side. "Thanks, Gary. For everything."

"You got it. Good luck, Joanie. *With* everything." Gary waved through the window at her and honked the horn as he drove away.

CHAPTER EIGHTEEN

Joanie had never in her life had a longer week. Nothing was different in her routine; she got up in the morning, ran for the bus, sat through her classes, did her homework. But nothing felt right. She felt detached, and sort of outside of it all, as if she were just floating along. She didn't care about any of it.

She couldn't even draw. Not one cartoon, not one spiky-haired figure, not one single frame of anything all week. Her pencil would hover over blank paper and eventually she would get bored and turn on the TV or go to sleep.

And to make it all worse, Zane and Samantha were hanging out together again. Joanie didn't object to them dating, if that was what they were doing, she didn't object at all. She was happy for Zane, or she tried to be, as much as she could be happy about anything right now. But really, it just made her more depressed.

Kate hadn't spoken to her all week. Or, well, to be fair, Kate had tried, and Joanie had walked away. Twice. So maybe it was more than Joanie hadn't let Kate talk to her. Either way, things were uncomfortable.

Finally, on Friday afternoon during X-period, Kate found Joanie in the library. She sat down at the table with Joanie and tossed a note onto Joanie's book. Joanie wanted to ignore it, but it was sitting right in the middle of her page so there was no way to pretend she didn't see the thing. She glanced up at Kate.

"What is this?" she whispered.

"A note," Kate answered casually.

"Why are you writing me notes?"

"Because, you don't listen when I talk. And it's important."

"Joanie looked down at the note, then back up at Kate, then picked up the note and opened it.

Dear Joanie, it read. *Will you please go to the prom with me? Love, Kate*

Joanie snorted and shook her head. "You've got to be kidding."

"No, actually," Kate said, leaning back in her chair. "I wasn't kidding. I'm not."

"We can't go to the prom together, Kate."

"Why not?"

Joanie raised an eyebrow. "Come on, you know why."

"I can't think of a single reason, Joanie. I want you to go with me."

"I'm not even sure I want to go at all."

"Look," Kate sighed. "I don't need an answer right now, okay? I'm not going to take no for an answer, yet. You think about it, decide what you want to do and you let me know on Monday."

"On Monday?"

"Yes, thank you." Kate stood up. "Do you have weekend plans?"

"Well, no. Not really."

"Call me."

"...okay." Joanie blinked at Kate. "Okay."

That night, with Kate's note open in front of her, Joanie was finally able to put something down in her journal.

Love, Kate, she wrote in big letters across the top of the page. *Love, Kate,* she scribbled up the side margin. *Love, Kate,* she wrote diagonally across the paper. She didn't stop until the page was filled with the phrase, the words overlapping and becoming illegible.

Love

And finally, after a week of feeling nothing, after a week of being numb and removed and tired, Joanie felt something. But it wasn't what she wanted to feel at all. What she was feeling wasn't love or excitement; it was fear.

There was absolutely no way that she could go to the prom and dance in front of the entire class with Kate. No way. She wasn't brave enough, and it wasn't fair of Kate to ask her. No.

No. She'd tell Kate on Monday. Joanie crumpled the note and threw it into the trash.

But she pulled it out again before she went to bed and stuck it in her journal.

CHAPTER NINETEEN

Homework took priority on Saturday. It didn't really need to, but it was distracting, and now that Joanie had plugged back into her feelings about Kate, she was having a hard time thinking about anything else. She did her math homework first, including the extra credit problem that wasn't due until the following Friday. She read her English homework and flipped through her history book until she figured out what she wanted to write the essay portion of her final exam about.

By three in the afternoon she ran out of work to do and went looking for Liz.

"What are you doing?"

Liz looked up from where she was sitting on the floor, the controller to her PS3 in her hands. "What's it look like?" she asked sarcastically, as any sister would.

"Can I play, too?"

"It's only for one player, at a time, Jo." Liz rolled her eyes, pausing the game and looking at Joanie to make it clear Joanie was interrupting.

"Okay," Joanie shrugged and wandered off again, winding up in the kitchen where her mother was giving the spaghetti sauce a stir. The house always smelled good on Saturdays, like garlic and oregano. Joanie opened the refrigerator door.

"Hungry?" her mother asked.

"Not really."

"What are you looking for?"

Joanie shrugged. "I don't know." She shut the door again.

"Everything okay, honey?"

"Yeah. Yep. Fine." Joanie tried to flee the kitchen, not wanting to get into a conversation with her mother, but the doorbell rang.

"Can you get that, Jo?" her mom asked, adding something to the sauce pot.

"Oh. Sure."

It was a brilliantly sunny day and Joanie was assaulted by beams of bright sunlight when she opened the door. It made her squint to see who was there, silhouetted against the sun.

"Hi, Joanie."

Joanie blinked and squinted again, but her there was nothing wrong with her vision, it really was Kate.

"Who is it, Jo?"

"It's," Joanie called back. "It's my uh, my friend Kate. You know, from school?" Joanie stepped to the side so Kate's head was blocking the sunlight and whispered, "What are you doing here?"

"Okay." Joanie's mother called back.

Kate shrugged. "Wanted to see you."

"You didn't call."

"You'd have made up some excuse about homework

or something."

"I would not!" Joanie protested, but part of her knew Kate was right. She still had knots in her stomach from the night before.

"Aren't you going to invite Kate in, Joanie?"

Joanie looked at Kate, who smiled back at Joanie; her smile was even brighter than the rays of sun in Joanie's eyes. "Yeah, aren't you going to invite me in?" Kate winked. Joanie stepped back from the door.

"You wanna come in?"

"I do." Kate stepped inside, took the door handle from Joanie and closed the front door behind her.

There was nothing to be done, you had to cut through the kitchen to get anywhere in the house, so Joanie led Kate inside. "Mom, this is Kate."

"Hello, Kate. How are you?"

"I'm fine, Mrs. Pierce." Kate answered politely.

"Good. School is going okay? Are you all caught up?"

"Oh, yeah. I'm fine now."

"Great. Well, it's nice to meet you finally." Joanie's mom went back to her sauce.

There was an awkward moment of silence, both Kate and Joanie looking at the floor, at each other, and then back to the floor. Joanie's mom turned around again.

"Why don't you two head on upstairs? I'll bring some munchies in a little while."

Joanie glanced up at her mother, then at Kate, then walked past Kate toward the stairs. "Okay." She wasn't sure alone time with Kate was what she wanted right now, but what was she going to say?

Kate followed, and when Joanie closed her door behind them, she said, "I can go if you want."

136

Joanie sighed, relenting a bit, trying to smile. "No, no. You can't leave now, Mom's making *munchies*."

Kate laughed softly. "'kay."

Joanie sat on the end of her bed and watched Kate look around her room. "Those pictures are from our ninth grade outing," she told Kate. "It was one of those 'get to know your classmates' things where you fall backwards off platforms and hope people catch you and stuff."

"Trust exercises," Kate added with a nod.

"Something like that."

"Zane looks really young in this picture."

"Oh, yeah. He had such a baby face freshman year. He was so cute."

"He is still cute."

"He is, but different cute."

Kate nodded. "Different cute. The girls are really into him."

"Oh, my God, yes."

"Who is the blonde he's been hanging out with?"

"Samantha? They used to go out."

"They broke up?"

Joanie nodded. "Yep."

"Isn't he taking her to the prom?"

"Yeah, he said he asked her."

Kate looked at Joanie. "So they're back together?"

Joanie shrugged and snorted. "Who knows?"

Kate wandered the room a little more, looking at Joanie's things. Mementos from her seventh grade Earth Day project, her brief second grade stint in the Girl Scouts, last summer's rafting camp. Finally, she turned around and looked at Joanie.

"I didn't mean to make things awkward and horrible between us."

"Things aren't horrible."

"Yes, they are."

"Okay, maybe a little."

Kate laughed softly and smiled again. "See?" she asked, and Joanie had to laugh back.

"I'm sorry I'm so..."

"I really like you, Joanie. That's what I came here to tell you. I really like you."

"I..." Joanie heart was doing that crazy beating thing in her chest again and she stood up as Kate stepped closer. "I'm scared."

"I know." Kate kissed her softy. "It's okay."

Joanie searched Kate's eyes. "It is?"

"Well, I'd still like you to come to the prom with me, though..."

"I can't."

"I know. It's a shame you're going to miss it, though."

"No, I mean, I'm not going to miss it. I am going with someone else." That sounded so horrible that Joanie was instantly ashamed of herself.

Kate blinked at her and took a step back. "Oh. You are?"

"I'm going with... a kid named Liam Andrews." Joanie looked at the floor.

"Why?"

"Because!" Joanie flopped on the end of her bed again. "I needed a date and my parents set me up, okay?"

"You'd rather go with some guy you barely know than with me?" Kate's voice was softer than usual.

"No! But Kate, we can't go to the prom together."

"Yes, Joanie, we can."

"No, we can't. People will--"

"People will what? Talk? Call you a lesbian? Make fun of us?"

"Yes!"

"So what?"

Joanie shook her head. "I'm going with Liam."

Kate raised an eyebrow. "And you won't even consider going with me."

"Kate, we can still hang out, we can still see each other. It's just a prom." But it was more than just a prom for Kate; Joanie could see that. She looked hurt. Joanie stood up again, trying to think of what to say to fix it.

Kate shook her head. "I hope you have a good time."

"You're going to go, aren't you?"

"No."

"Kate..."

Joanie's mom knocked on the door. "Hey ladies, I have snacks!" she called through the door.

"I gotta go."

"Kate, wait!" Joanie called after her, but she was already opening Joanie's bedroom door. She stepped around Joanie's mom and ran down the stairs leaving Joanie to stare after her.

"Joanie?"

"'m not hungry." Joanie closed the door again.

"Joanie, are you okay?" her mom called through the door.

"Leave me alone!" was all Joanie could manage to say before bursting into tears.

CHAPTER
TWENTY

Joanie looked at herself in the mirror, wearing a strapless bra and panty hose. Her hair was smoothed down but still kind of funky and modern looking, pulled at an angle across her forehead. Her mom had done her make-up, and miraculously, they'd agreed on everything including the lipstick color.

All that was left was to put on the dress and her shoes.

"Joanie? Do you need help?" her mom asked, poking her head in the door.

"Zip me?" Joanie hurried over to where the dress lay on her bed and pulled the top on. She probably could have zipped it up herself, but her mom had been hovering for a while and she figured it was best to give her something to do.

"Of course." Her mom smiled and hurried into the room. She zipped up the back for Joanie, and then reached for the skirt, holding it open for Joanie to step in.

"You're going to have such fun."

"I hope so."

"My first prom was unforgettable; I know yours will be, too."

Joanie was pretty sure no matter what happened tonight she wasn't going to forget it.

They got the skirt on and Joanie stepped into her shoes, just in time to hear the doorbell ring.

"I'll get it." Her mom hurried from the room, and Joanie wondered if she wasn't having more fun with this than Joanie was. A few minutes later, as Joanie had expected, her mom called upstairs. "Joanie honey, Liam is here."

Joanie looked at herself in the mirror. She barely recognized herself, really; the heels and the hair, everything made her look so different. She stepped side to side as if dancing to see what her skirt would do and smiled as it swished around her ankles. Her mom had been right about the skirt after all, it was beautiful.

The doorbell rang again. "Oh, that'll be Zane. Joanie! Come on, honey!" her mom called again and Joanie sighed. It was time.

She made her way down the stairs and found Liam waiting in the living room. He looked handsome, she had to admit. He had on a black tux, with a classic lack tie and cummerbund, and shiny black shoes. His brown hair was combed neatly and framed a very handsome face set with hazel eyes and straight, white teeth that showed when he smiled.

"Hi," she said, more shyly than she had intended.

"Hello." Liam held out a corsage.

"Oh, uh, thank you." Joanie held out her wrist and Liam tied it on for her. He didn't seem nervous at all, and tied it on neatly.

"You look really pretty," Liam told her.

"Joanie! Zane and Samantha are here and the limo looks... oh, my. You two look wonderful together." Joanie blushed and her mom ran for the camera.

"Hey," Zane said, leaning in to kiss Joanie on the cheek.

"Hi. Hello, Samantha."

"Hi, Joanie."

Samantha looked beautiful. Her dress was delicate and feminine and flowed around her, making her look like a goddess. Or an angel. And Zane looked great, too. Joanie smiled at them both.

"Pictures!" her mother called, and they all groaned.

"Oh, hush. You'll want them later, trust me."

They posed and smiled for a series of pictures as couples, as a foursome, just the girls, just the boys, and then Zane took a few of Joanie and her mom. Finally, the limo beeped at them and it was time to go.

"Dude," Liam said as the limo drove off. "What was up with your mom and the pictures?"

"Sorry about that," Joanie said, shrugging. "That's just mom."

Zane laughed. "Samantha's mom brought her over to my house and took a million pictures, too."

"Must be a girl thing. My mom was like, 'be home by midnight or you're grounded', and pushed me out the door."

Joanie laughed. "Oh, I wish."

142

The prom was being held at a local hotel, and the limo pulled up right in front to let them out. Both Zane and Liam offered their arms and Samantha and Joanie were escorted into the prom in style.

There was a stage at one end of the room where a band was set up to play, but the music was being piped in and no one was on stage yet. The lighting was in rich reds and blues and there were a couple of mirror balls sending little bubbles of white light around the room. There were tons of people there already and more filing in behind Joanie and Liam, and camera flashes were going off everywhere. Joanie hadn't thought to bring a camera, but she had a feeling she wasn't going to need pictures to remind her of anything.

A man walked by with a tray and lowered it in front of them. "Mini-quiche?" he asked, offering them some. Zane took two, everyone else passed.

"Pig," Joanie teased.

Zane laughed. "I'm hungry!"

"He's a bottomless pit," Samantha chimed in.

"Great, just what I need, two of you teasing me."

"Just like old times," Joanie sang. Samantha laughed and Zane rolled his eyes.

Liam cleared his throat. "So... what do you want to do? Dance?"

"Why don't we figure out where we're supposed to sit?" Zane suggested gesturing to the tables that were set up at the far end of the room.

"Sounds good." Liam headed off in that direction and Joanie followed.

Their seats turned out to be right in the middle of

everything. They had a clear view of the band, an easy walk to the buffet, and they were surrounded by other tables, which mean they could socialize and gossip, too. Zane was thrilled, he loved to people watch. While Samantha and Joanie claimed their seats, Zane and Liam went to get everyone something to drink.

"So," Joanie asked to Samantha, once the boys were gone. "You two are...?"

"Yeah. Back together. I think."

"That's great." Joanie wasn't convinced it was, but she never really understood why they broke up to begin with.

"It is. He's sweet. He's always been really... sweet to me. Nice. A gentleman."

Joanie smiled. "He's a good guy."

"What about Liam? How did you two meet?"

"Oh, Liam is... I don't know him at all. I just met him tonight."

"You're kidding!"

"Nope. I... didn't have a date. My dad set me up."

"Well, he's good looking. You could have done worse."

"I guess."

"Hopefully he's a good dancer."

"I hope." Joanie loved to dance; it was most of the reason she really wanted to go to the prom in the first place.

"One Cherry Coke," Zane said, setting a glass in front of Samantha. Liam put Joanie's Sprite down in front of her.

"Thanks."

"No problem."

***

Everyone thought dinner was pretty good. They had a choice of chicken or beef, rice, pasta, salad and green beans – nothing scary and everything seemed to be cooked well. It was served buffet style, and by the time Joanie got back to the table her plate was loaded.

"I'm never going to eat all of this," she told Samantha, whose plate was similarly full.

"Me neither, but I couldn't decide!"

"Exactly!"

Liam and Zane's plates were even worse. In fact, Liam had two. It was just as well that he kept his mouth full because, as she had feared, he and Joanie had absolutely nothing to talk about. Joanie didn't watch football, she didn't understand football, she didn't *like* football. Liam seemed to eat, sleep, and breathe the sport. Liam liked pop music, Joanie listened to alternative. Joanie liked to read, Liam... didn't. Zane did his best to keep the conversation going and include Liam, but at some point even he gave up. He just wasn't a jock.

It wasn't until after dinner that Joanie discovered that there was one thing she and Liam did have in common. She was thrilled when Liam hopped up as soon as the band started playing.

"You wanna dance?" he asked, leaning toward the dance floor.

"Love to," Joanie answered and hurried after him as he led the way.

It didn't matter what they were listening to, they both loved to dance. And Liam was good at it. They danced separately to the faster songs and together for the more traditional ones because Liam actually knew how to lead. They even slow-danced, which Joanie used as a moment to catch her breath. She never once thought of it as anything even vaguely romantic, especially when all Liam could talk about now that they were away from the table was Samantha.

"She's hot, huh?"

Okay, so she and Liam had something else in common. They both thought Samantha was gorgeous.

"She's pretty, yeah."

"Zane's seriously lucky. She left Dave Arch for him, you know."

"She was with Zane before David," Joanie corrected. "And she and David were never dating really."

Liam snorted. "That's not what David said."

"You believe everything a..." Joanie stopped herself. 'Everything a stupid, brainless, jock tells you' would not be a good thing to say right now. "Everything people say?"

"I believe Dave; he had details."

Joanie didn't. But she kept on dancing.

Eventually, though, even she had to admit she was tired. Liam went off to get sodas and Joanie headed for their table. Zane and Samantha weren't there, so she sat by herself waiting for Liam to get back.

"Wanna get some air?" Liam gestured to the back door with the hand that had her Sprite in it.

"Yeah, okay." It was stuffy inside with everyone dancing and someone had propped open the back door to let in some cool air. The night was lovely, still cool but not cold, and there was a nice breeze. The sky was completely clear. "Look at all the stars," Joanie remarked, and sipped her Sprite.

"Yep. Nice night."

"Are you having a good time?"

"Sure."

"I mean, I know I'm probably boring you because I don't know anything about football and I'm kind of..."

"You're a great dancer. You follow a lead really well."

"Yeah?" Joanie looked up at Liam.

"Yeah. Most girls just want to dance by themselves."

Joanie smiled. She wasn't 'most girls', that much she knew. Usually, it didn't seem like that was a good thing, so it was nice to hear Liam say he liked that she was different.

But that didn't make her ready for the arm that Liam wrapped around her waist.

"You want to go back in and dance?"

"No." Liam took the Sprite from her hand and set it on a ledge next to his Coke.

"Uh, no?" Joanie swallowed. She hadn't seen this coming at all and now she wasn't sure how to politely get out of it. Liam's arm tightened around her and he leaned in closer.

"Can I kiss you?" he asked. He asked nicely even, but he didn't seem to be waiting for a reply.

"I... uh..."

Liam kissed her gently and Joanie was so startled that all she could do was blink until he pulled away. Okay, she thought, one kiss, no big deal. It actually made her think of Kate, and how much she'd rather be with Kate right now.

"You look amazing, Joanie," Liam said, throwing a compliment in to woo her.

"Let's go back inside, okay?"

"Sure you don't want to stay out here a little longer?" Liam smiled and leaned in for another kiss.

"Liam..." Joanie wasn't sure what to do and she put

her hands up on his chest. He kissed her again and she made a soft noise in protest.

Liam pulled back a little. "What? It's just a kiss, Joanie."

"Don't want to." Suddenly, she wanted to go home. Her chest felt tight and her stomach was churning.

"Okay." Liam looked confused. "We can go back inside and dance if you want."

"NO!" Joanie screamed in his face. She pushed him away and he didn't try hold on, letting her go so abruptly that she stumbled backwards a step. But Joanie felt a strange rush of adrenaline and she just couldn't stop herself. Her head swam and emotion poured out of her. She reached out and slapped Liam in the face.

Hard.

"Ow!" Liam shouted. "What the hell is wrong with you?"

"Go away!" Joanie screamed, and the next thing she knew her fists were flying, hitting Liam in the shoulders and chest. He started to back away, but she just went after him.

Liam was shouting back at her and trying to shove her away. "Jesus Christ, you're crazy!"

Joanie felt herself breathing hard and hot tears were streaming down her face. She was dimly aware that a crowd had started to form around them and people crowded in the doorway, too. She heard her name being called over and over, but it sounded far away and weirdly distorted. Eventually though, and she couldn't remember how it happened, she realized that she was hitting Zane and not Liam.

Zane took her by the shoulders. "Joanie!" He shouted in her face and gave her a hard shake.

That time, Joanie heard him.

A deep voice sounded firm and loud behind her. "What is going on out here?" the voice demanded.

"That chick is crazy," Liam said and walked past the chaperone into the building.

"Is everyone okay?" It was Mr. Foster. Joanie finally recognized him as she was starting to calm down. She leaned into Zane and Zane put his arms around her.

"I'm sorry," she told Mr. Foster. She didn't know what else to say. "I'm sorry."

"Are you okay, Joanie?" Mr. Foster was looking at her seriously.

"I'm okay," she told him, not really knowing if it was true or not. "I just want to go home." She looked at Zane who nodded at her. Samantha was hovering over Zane's shoulder uncertainly. "I'm sorry, Samantha."

Mr. Foster handed Zane a card. "Have her parents call me if they want to. I'm going to see if I can find Liam."

"Not his fault," Joanie said quickly. "Mr. Foster? It's not his fault. Okay?"

Mr. Foster looked at Joanie for a long moment and then nodded. "Okay, Joanie. I'm just going to go see if he's all right."

Once Mr. Foster left, the crowd of students started to disappear and the party went on inside. Joanie sat with Zane on a bench against the side of the building, tugging at the handkerchief that he'd given her, worrying it between her fingers. She couldn't seem to stop crying.

"Are you ready to go home?" Zane asked her finally.

"No."

"Joanie..."

"My parents are going to flip out." Joanie sighed. "I shouldn't have come."

"Joanie, don't say that. You were having fun for a while."

"I shouldn't have come with Liam."

Zane covered her hands with his. "You didn't know he was going to be a jerk."

"No!" Joanie protested, grabbing his hands. "That's just it, Zane. He wasn't a jerk. I mean, yeah, he tried to kiss me, but he wasn't a jerk."

"They why—"

"I don't know. I just... flipped out on him." Joanie closed her eyes, thinking back on what happened, trying to remember anything she could but it was kind of a blur. "He kissed me once and then I was thinking about Kate and I got upset and totally... lost it."

"Shit."

"Yeah. And now I have to go home and..."

"Are you okay, Jo?"

"I don't know," Joanie replied truthfully. "I feel kind of funny."

"Funny?" Zane glanced at Samantha as she came back outside. "Like faint, funny?"

"No, I'm not going to faint."

"Your parents are here."

Joanie's eyes widened. "What? Oh, no..." Mr. Foster must have called them.

"Joanie? Joanie honey?" Joanie's mom came running out the door. Samantha stepped back out of the way. "Joanie!"

There was a bit of a commotion, and the next thing Joanie knew she was being bundled into her dad's car. Zane and Samantha got in the backseat with her. Her parents asked a lot of questions as they drove but Zane stepped up and answered everything for Joanie, and she just stared out the window as they drove Samantha home. He explained about Liam and everything – he was the best friend anyone could ever want to have. And after Samantha got out of the car and Zane walked her inside, he came running back out and got back in the car with Joanie.

"Shouldn't you—"

"We're going to talk tomorrow."

Joanie shook her head. "But she's your—"

"I'm here for you Joanie, okay?"

Joanie smiled. It was a small one, but as she thought about Zane putting her first, taking care of her when he had a girlfriend he should be spending time with, it just made her feel so happy she couldn't help but smile a little. It made her feel loved. She snuggled into his side and put her head on his shoulder.

CHAPTER TWENTY ONE

Sleeping was pretty much out of the question.

Joanie's mom stuck her in a hot shower when they got home, to wash all the gunk out of her hair and the make-up off her face. The water felt good, and it should have made Joanie relaxed and sleepy. She got into her pajamas and let Zane fuss over her and tuck her in. Her dad brought Zane a t-shirt and sweats and Joanie's sleeping bag. Zane climbed right into it and snuggled down with a yawn.

"Goodnight, Jo," he said softly. "Tomorrow will be better."

"I hope so. Goodnight, Z."

Zane was snoring almost instantly, but an hour later, Joanie was still lying awake in bed and her stomach was growling. She peered over the bed to look at Zane and all she could see of him was a tuft of hair on the very top of his head. Everything else was buried in the sleeping bag.

He'd slept like that as long as Joanie had known him.

Quietly, Joanie slipped out of bed, wiggling her feet into the red Elmo slippers that Liz had given her for Christmas and pulling on her bathrobe. The house was dark, but Joanie knew the stairs well, taking the top two on the far right so they didn't squeak and the bottom three stepping only on the front edge.

From there the going was easy, with the light from the street spilling in through the kitchen window. She really wanted popcorn, but the microwave would wake up her parents so she got a glass of milk and a strawberry frosted Pop-Tart from the pantry and headed into the living room where she could snuggle into the couch under her mother's chenille throw.

Kate was on her mind, and something Kate had said, about how Joanie would rather go to the prom with some guy she didn't know than go with a girl. When it came down to it, yes, Joanie admitted to herself, it was easier to do what she did than do what she wanted to do. It was easier, but it wasn't right. Not for her.

Hours after the prom was over, Joanie had a much better idea of what had happened to her at the prom, but still no idea what to do about it. Until her dad sat down on the couch with her.

"Hey," he said, taking a bite of a sandwich.

"Peanut butter?" Joanie asked, smelling it.

"Yup."

"No pie, huh?" Joanie smiled and leaned on him a little.

"Nope. We're out." Her dad put his arm around her shoulders and they both sighed.

"What are you doing up?" Joanie asked.

"I couldn't sleep."

"Me neither."

"Your mom and I are worried about you."

Joanie nodded. "Yeah. I can see why."

"It's more than tonight, Joanie," he said, and took another bite of his sandwich. When he spoke again, his words were muffled by a mouth full of peanut butter. "You been weally unhappy lade-ly."

"You noticed, huh?"

Her dad nodded rather than talking this time.

"Yeah, well. You're right. Or, you're half right, actually. I have been really unhappy, but I've been really happy, too."

"Okay." Her dad looked at her, just accepting her statement as fact and not pushing. "You want to talk about it?"

"No," Joanie said automatically. But just as her dad was nodding in understanding, she impulsively changed her mind. "Yes."

"Yes?" Her dad looked back at her quickly. "You do?"

"Yes. Yes, I do. I do want to talk about it because I need to... I have something I... need to tell you." This was totally unrehearsed, and the few things she had thought about or even practiced saying were not coming to mind. She was winging it, and it was both scary and also, somehow, not.

"Okay, sweetheart, you can, uh, you can tell me anything you want." Her dad suddenly looked weirdly nervous. "I hope you know that."

"I'm not pregnant, Dad," Joanie said quickly.

"Oh, thank God." Her dad flopped backwards against the couch with a dramatic gesture.

"Dad!"

"I mean, I'd support you, you know I would, Jo, but… damn. That's a relief."

Joanie reached out and slapped him playfully.

"Hey, hey now. Haven't you punched enough men tonight?"

"Ha ha ha." She crossed her arms over her chest and sank back into the couch. "I totally ruined my prom, Dad, that's not funny.

"Nah. You know, I threw a few punches at my prom, too."

"What?"

"Oh, yeah. I never told you that story?"

Joanie looked at him. "No. Were you dating Mom?"

"Oh, God, no. I didn't meet your mom until college."

"Oh, right." Joanie nodded.

"It was a couple of weeks before the prom and I still didn't have a date. Well, I *had* a girlfriend, but she broke up with me a couple of weeks before."

"That sucks."

"Yeah. Women."

Joanie snorted.

"Anyway, so I met this girl at the library and I liked her. Then, when I ran into her a week later, I asked her if she wanted to go to my prom with me. She went to a different school so her prom was another weekend. Anyway, she said sure."

"Okay." Joanie had no idea where her dad was going with this.

"So it's the night of the prom and I pick her up – her name was Allison, I remember now – anyway, so I pick her up and we go to the prom. She looked great, pretty dress, her hair was perfect, and I was in teenage boy heaven."

"Dad, are you making this up to make me feel better?"

"What?"

"Like you did when I forgot my lines in the fourth grade musical?"

"I didn't make that up!"

"Dad…"

"Okay, fine. I did make that up but it made you feel better."

Joanie smiled. "It did."

"But I'm not making this up. Promise."

"Okay," Joanie smiled.

"So, okay, we're at the prom and we've been there like an hour and we're dancing and this guy comes up to us. He's wearing blue jeans and a button down shirt and he starts talking to Allison. He says, "What are you doing?", and she says, "Go away, Teddy, I'm dancing." And I'm trying to figure out what is going on so I ask the guy who he is."

"Uh-oh," Joanie turned in her seat to see her dad better.

"Yeah, big time uh-oh. He looks at me and he says, "I'm her boyfriend, who are *you*?"

"Oh, crap!"

"Right. And I realize that I am a stud *now*," he said and grinned at Joanie, "but I was a skinny nerd in high school, and this guy picked me right up off the floor and shoved me."

"What did you do?"

"Well, Allison started crying and ran over to me, and I stood up, marched over to him and punched him in the face."

"Woo!"

"Heh. You say that, but I didn't win that fight. They ended up breaking us up, they threw us all out and I got suspended. I got a ride home in a police car and when your grandfather got a look at my bloody nose and swollen lip, he was *not* happy with me."

"Grandpa?"

"Oh, yeah. I thought he was going to *kill* me. He didn't quite, but I was grounded forever. I was a hero in school, though."

Joanie laughed. "Did you ever see Allison again?"

"Yep. She came by the next day to apologize and we dated for a little while but it didn't really work out."

"Poor Daddy." Joanie patter his hand.

"Poor Daddy, nothing," her mom said from the doorway. "He got me."

"Lucky, lucky you," her dad said sarcastically. They all laughed.

"Seems like none of us is sleeping, huh?"

Joanie put a finger in the air in correction. "Except Zane, he's snoring."

"You're lucky to have him, Jo."

Joanie just nodded. "He rocks."

"So, uh… I did all the talking," her dad pointed out, "but you were the one who wanted to talk, huh?"

Then her mother did something she'd never done before. "Oh, I'm sorry, you two. Let me just get my tea and I'll head on back to bed."

"No wait, Mom," Joanie said, calling her mom back into the room. "Come sit."

She saw the look her parents exchanged but didn't comment on it.

"She's not pregnant," he father added quickly.

"Ah. Good. Great."

"You two thought I was...?"

"Mood swings, weird eating habits, hiding in your room..."

"Oh, God. I'm not pregnant you guys, I'm just gay."

"Oh, well then, that's..." her mother's reaction was almost comical. Joanie would have laughed but she was too busy being stunned that's she'd just blurted it out like that. "Wait. What?"

"Kate? You know Kate?"

"Yes," her dad said carefully. "We know Kate."

"She's my girlfriend." Hopefully. Assuming she hadn't ruined everything with the whole prom thing.

"Kate." Her mother nodded her head looking a little stunned and Joanie suddenly realized that her mom had no idea what to do with what Joanie had just told her. But her dad seemed a little steadier.

"She's pretty."

Joanie smiled. "She is. And smart, and kind, and..." Joanie sighed.

"Is this like," her dad started to ask and the changed his question a little. "How serious are you about her?"

"I... think... I think love her, Dad."

"Wow."

Joanie nodded. "That's kind of how I feel." She looked over at her mom who had sunk down into a chair. "I'm okay, Mom."

"Zane knows?"

Joanie nodded. "Yeah, Dad, he does." She knew her mom was going to be the one with issues, her dad rolled with the punches pretty well. Well, he did now but apparently didn't as a teenager. "Mom?"

Her mom looked up at her. "We love you, Joanie, you know that, right?"

Joanie smiled. "Yeah, I know, Mom."

"So, it's okay if I think about this a little?"

Joanie nodded. "Yeah, it's okay. I've had years to think about it, you've had five minutes."

Her mom smiled and Joanie got up and hugged her. "Will you still love me if I'm suspended from school for beating up Liam?"

She felt her mom laugh against her but her dad said, "We'll love you. And you'll love mowing the lawn for a month."

Joanie groaned. "I guess I'd better get my rest, then," Joanie said with a yawn. She was exhausted all of a sudden and her pillow was calling her. Plus, it seemed like maybe her parents needed to talk.

"Good idea, Jo." Her dad got up and gave her an enormous bear hug, pet her hair and then let her go. "I love you, sweetheart. We all need some rest. Everything will be okay."

"Thanks, Dad. Night. Night, Mom."

"Goodnight, Jo."

Joanie felt a thousand times lighter as she climbed the stairs, but she was so tired she was practically asleep before her head hit the pillow.

CHAPTER

TWENTY TWO

When Joanie woke up Sunday morning it was well after lunch time. She hauled herself out of bed, dressed in jeans and a T-shirt and made her way downstairs. She had two thoughts in her head. One, she was starving, and two, she couldn't believe how late she'd slept. But when she neared the bottom of the stairs and heard Zane's voice in the kitchen, everything from the night before came flooding back to her.

"All I can tell you is that he couldn't talk about anything but football. He was a complete snore."

"Was he nice, at least?"

Joanie groaned and headed into the kitchen.

"Oh, yeah. He got Jo drinks and danced with her and stuff. He was nice enough, I guess."

"We had nothing to talk about, Mom. I told you we'd have nothing to talk about," Joanie said, barging in on the conversation. She was trying to sound annoyed, but it didn't last long. From the looks of things, everyone was up late and having a late lunch, and her mom had made Joanie's favorite. "Oh, my God. Mac and cheese."

"Just for you, sweetheart." Her mom got up and went right to the stove.

"Good morning, you," her father said, smiling from across the kitchen table.

"Hey, Sleeping Beauty." Zane got up and hugged her. "How did you sleep?"

"Not so well at first," Joanie said, hugging him back. "And then like a rock later."

"Yeah, they told me."

"I figured."

"Congratulations." Zane pulled her over to the table and poured her a glass of coke from the bottle on the table. "You should wear rainbow colors today or something. A big fat sign on your back that says 'I Kiss Girls'."

"I wouldn't necessarily go that far," her mom said, setting a big bowl of mac and cheese down in front of Joanie.

Joanie laughed. "No, me neither." She looked at Zane. "I might go see Kate, though."

"Oh, you should." Zane nodded. "You totally should."

"Joanie," her father chimed in, "do Kate's parents know about Kate?"

"Yes."

Her dad nodded. "Cool, okay. And, do they know about you?"

Joanie blushed. "Her mom knows. Kate kind of outed me by mistake."

"I bet her mom knew anyway, you know, deep in her heart? Mothers always know these things. I knew, I mean

I had my suspicions and—"

"Sure, Carol," her dad said playfully. "You said it was hormones."

"I wasn't wrong," her mom protested. "And *you* thought she was pregnant."

"I've never been so happy to be wrong in all my life," her dad said, grinning broadly.

"Well, that won't happen at least," Zane said, cheerfully. Both of Joanie's parents shot him a look and his eyes grew wide. "That is..." he went on, tripping over his own tongue. "...if she were to decide to... I mean, not that she has but... it's something to..." Zane sighed. "Man, this mac and cheese is awesome."

Joanie laughed, and Zane stuffed his mouth before he could say another word. "You see why I love him," she said to her dad.

"Hey, I saw that last night."

Joanie smiled. "Yeah. Thanks, Zane. I don't know what I would have done if you hadn't been there."

"You'd have beat the crap out of Andrews."

"You're probably right. Oh, God. I'm so going to be suspended or something."

"No, you're not. We talked with Mr. Foster and your dad called Liam's father..."

Joanie gasped. "You didn't!"

"Yes, I did. Parents do that sort of thing."

Joanie hid behind a bite of macaroni.

"Anyway, things are fine. You didn't even hurt Liam as it turns out; you just freaked him out a little."

"I freaked myself out a little."

"I have a bruise you know." Zane pulled his T-shirt sleeve up, and sure enough, there was a small purple bruise there. "Right here." He tried to pout, which was so adorable, Joanie couldn't help herself.

"Aw."

Zane grinned at her.

"Wimp."

Her dad laughed.

Joanie put down her fork. "Okay, you need to go spend some time with your date from last night, and I need to get cleaned up, and then I need to go try to talk to Kate."

"Try to?" her mom asked.

Joanie and Zane looked at each other. Zane talked first. "They kind of broke up last week."

"We didn't break up. We're just… not speaking right now."

Joanie's parents exchanged a look next. "Okay, honey," her dad said. "Go on and do what you gotta do."

"Thanks, Dad!" Joanie and Zane got up.

"Call me later," Zane said. "Let me know how it went."

Joanie nodded. "Will do. Hug Samantha for me? And tell her I'm sorry."

"I'll tell her."

Joanie rang Kate's doorbell. It was a while before anyone answered but her mom finally came to the door.

"Oh, hello, Joanie," Mrs. Dalton said, looking a little uncomfortable.

"Hi, Mrs. Dalton. Is Kate around?"

"Actually, no. She's out shopping with her dad right now."

"Oh." Joanie nodded. "Okay. Well."

"How was the prom?"

Joanie wasn't sure if Mrs. Dalton was actually being kind or sarcastic. "It sucked."

"I'm sorry."

"I should have gone with Kate."

Mrs. Dalton smiled. "Can I leave her a message for you?"

"Um... just tell her I stopped by, and—wait a minute, actually, could I leave her a note?"

"Of course. Come on in."

In the kitchen Mrs. Dalton handed Joanie some paper and a pencil.

The first thing that Joanie did was draw a picture of a doghouse with feet sticking out through the door. Then she chewed on the pencil while she decided what else to say.

Dear Kate, she wrote, finally. *I'm not going to apologize in this note because I want to do it in person. Love, Joanie*

And then she drew a picture of her comic book self carrying a huge sign that read, *I Kiss Girls.* It wasn't displayed on her back, but Zane would have been pleased anyway.

Chapter Twenty Three

Joanie would have given her right arm to stay home on Monday. But she knew that staying home just meant that she'd have to face everything when she went in on Tuesday instead, so what was the point? It might even make things worse.

"You'd think," she told herself as she dressed in a hurry, "that someone who wanted to make a good impression would get up a little early – or, you know, even on time for school, but no." She looked at herself in the mirror quickly. "Aw hell, why start now?" She winked at her reflection, grabbed her knapsack and ran out the door.

"Joanie!"

"Here I come!" Joanie called back, taking the last three stairs in one leap.

Liz was shaking her head. "Late again," she sang.

"Yep! Bye, Mom." Joanie grabbed a banana and ran out the door.

Zane was waiting, and the bus was just pulling up.

"Coming!" she shouted.

Zane stood in the doorway of the bus until she got there, then grinned at the bus driver as he got on. They flopped into a seat together.

"You didn't call me."

"I had a pile of homework, and then I fell asleep."

"Lazy," Zane winked. "How'd things go with Kate?"

"Oh, she wasn't home. I left a note."

Zane nodded. "Bummer."

"Zane, today is going to suck."

"I bet not."

Joanie looked at him.

"Well? How many of those juniors do we hang out with? Not many. So who cares of the other ones think you're a freak?"

Joanie started to hit him, but stopped herself. "Jerk."

Zane snorted. "Maybe you should take up boxing."

She did hit him that time.

In truth, Joanie didn't care about people thinking she was a freak. She didn't even really care if everyone knew she was gay. Not really. What she cared about was what Kate was going to say when she saw her. And she cared about what would happen if she ran into Liam in school. She did care a little about what Mr. Foster was going to say, too, and he was the one they ran into first, in homeroom.

"Morning, Foster," Zane said in his usual way as they walked past Mr. Foster's desk.

"Good morning, Zane." He looked at Joanie. "Good morning, Joanie."

"Morning," Joanie mumbled.

"Got a minute?"

Joanie looked at Zane, who winked at her, and then she walked slowly up to Mr. Foster's desk.

"Are you okay?"

"I'm fine."

"Good." Mr. Foster smiled at her. "I was worried about you."

Joanie looked down at his desk. "Look, I'm sorry about—"

Mr. Foster held up a hand. "No need to apologize. I'm just glad you're okay. And Liam, too." He winked.

"Yeah, I need to work on my left hook," Joanie joked, winking back.

As Joanie had expected, she ran into Kate at lunch. Actually, she didn't run into Kate, Kate came and found her, and sat down with Joanie and Zane to eat.

"Hey, guys."

Zane glanced at Joanie and then back at Kate. "Hey, Kate."

"So, I heard the prom was interesting."

"You know what, I just realized that I need to read my history homework." Zane stood up. "I'll see you in math, Jo."

"Uh, yeah." Joanie was both grateful he was leaving, and nervous.

"Hi, Kate."

Kate gave her a gentle smile. "Hi, Joanie. I got your note."

"Oh. Yeah."

"You're a pretty good artist."

"It's just a hobby."

"It could be more than a hobby."

"I didn't write it to impress you with my artistic abilities."

"I know." Kate leaned forward. "So, did you seriously deck Liam?"

"What? No! I didn't deck anyone. I slapped him." Joanie swallowed. "And... kind of pounded on him a little."

Kate laughed. "The rumor is that you beat the snot out of him."

"What?"

"He's denying it, of course, but that's what everyone is saying."

"Oh, God. I didn't beat him up, I just, freaked out and lost it after he tried to kiss me."

"Well, I for one am glad to hear that." Kate grinned and sipped water from a bottle.

"Kate, I'm really sorry. I should have accepted your invitation and gone with you."

"It might have caused less of a scandal," Kate winked.

"You're having too much fun with this."

"It's awesome. I can't help it."

"It was a disaster. I've never been so... I don't know. Upset. Stupid. Embarrassed. I feel like an idiot."

"Hey, don't worry about it. By next month they'll be back to talking about Britney Spears."

Joanie snorted. "Thanks."

They ate quietly for a few minutes. Joanie was working up to talking about coming out and her parents when Kate beat her to it.

"Did you really tell your parents?"

Joanie looked up from her lunch. "How did you..."

"Zane sent me a text message."

"The sneak."

"He's happy for you. And he... knows how I feel."

Joanie bit her lip and nodded. "He knows how I feel, too."

"Great, so I can go to him to find out."

"What? Shut up. You know I..."

"Yes?"

"Love you."

Kate smiled. "I do now."

"I'll try, okay? I don't think I'm ready to run laps around the school waving a pride flag, but I'll try to be... honest. Okay?"

"It's a start."

"I, uh... when I came by yesterday, to your house and all, I wanted to apologize," Joanie said seriously. "But I also wanted to ask you... out."

Kate raised an eyebrow. "Out?"

"On a date."

"A real date?"

"A real date."

Kate smiled. "Can I hold your hand?"

"Yes, if you want to."

"Can I kiss you in public?"

Joanie blushed hard. "Uh, well, yes. If you want to." The heat was creeping up her cheeks and into her ears. Her stupid ears always turned bright red when she blushed.

"Where are you taking me?"

"Well, the ice is gone, so not ice skating. I was thinking roller skating."

"Oh, my God. How geeky."

"Oh. Well if you don't want to.."

"No, I do. I love geeky. Saturday?"

Joanie nodded. "Saturday."

CHAPTER TWENTY FOUR

Saturday it poured rain. It was raining so hard that Joanie had difficulty seeing out her bedroom windows as she got dressed for the roller rink. There had better be some serious May flowers coming after all the rain they'd had this month.

She hadn't been to the roller rink in a couple of years, and she was really looking forward to it. Unlike the ice rink, she didn't have to bundle up, so she pulled on a pair of comfortable jeans and a bright pink T-shirt. Then she spent a few minutes in the mirror making her hair stick out just so.

Obviously, she wasn't going to be biking anywhere so she hurried downstairs to ask her dad for a ride.

"The roller rink?"

"Yes, Kate and I are going."

"You've patched things up with Kate?" her dad asked curiously.

"*Things* didn't really need patching up, dad." Joanie rolled her eyes. "It wasn't like that."

Her dad watched her carefully. "Okay."

"What?"

"Nothing."

"Can I get a ride, or what?"

"Yes. Hang on, let me get my keys."

Her dad left her standing in the garage. "Ready?" he asked when she came back.

"Yep."

Her dad tossed her the keys. "Let's go."

Joanie looked at the keys. "Your car?"

"Yep, get in."

Joanie unlocked the doors and got in. She spent a few minutes adjusting the mirrors and the seat, then put on her seatbelt. "Okay?"

"Yep. I'm buckled in, let's go."

Using the mirrors, Joanie slowly backed the car out of the garage, relieved when the nose finally cleared the door. She did a K-turn in the driveway so she didn't have to back out into the street.

"Nicely done."

"Thanks."

"I guess that Driver's Ed guy knew what he was doing."

"It's his job, Dad."

"I'd have taught you, but your mom wanted the school. You know how she is." She and her dad complained about how protective and particular her mom was all the time, but it was done with love. "You know how she is" was just another way of saying that Joanie's mom was nervous about Joanie learning to drive.

"Dad, it's okay. Gary was nice."

"Gary?" Her dad nodded. "Okay. Good."

They drove down the street in the rain. Joanie was driving slowly, and her dad seemed perfectly relaxed in the passenger seat.

"So, Joanie?"

Uh-oh. This wasn't going to be good.

"Yeah?"

"How long have you known you're gay?"

Joanie glanced briefly at her dad. "Uh. A while."

"What's a while?"

"Well, I've known for sure since, like, eighth grade."

"Yeah? When did you wonder?"

"Like fourth grade, but I didn't know what I wanted really, just that something was different."

"Wow."

Joanie nodded, breathing a little easier. That wasn't so bad.

"So, have you kissed a girl yet?"

So much for easy breathing. "Dad!"

Her dad looked at her. "You'd rather have this conversation with your mother?"

"God, no."

"So?"

Joanie sighed. "Yes. I have."

"Anything else?"

"Nope."

"But you'd tell us... if you...?"

"Yep."

"And you'd be careful."

"Yep."

"Kay."

"Kay."

How she managed not to drive off the road she'd never

know. But they made it to the rink in one piece despite the insanity both outside and inside the car.

"You need me to pick you up?"

"I don't know. I don't think so. I'll call you."

"Have fun. Say hi to Kate for us." Her dad blew a kiss at her and she smiled.

"Will do."

Kate was already in line for skates when Joanie found her.

"Shoe size?"

"Eight," Kate said.

"And six and a half," Joanie added.

"You have little feet!"

"I do not, yours are big." Joanie grinned at Kate.

They took their stuff over to the lockers and shared one, locking their things inside before sitting down to put on their skates.

"Can you believe the rain?" Kate asked.

"My dad asked me if I'd kissed you."

Kate nodded. "Much more interesting conversation than the weather. What did you tell him?"

"I told him yes."

"Good." Kate smiled. "Truth is good. Was he okay with it?"

"Yeah, I think so. He seemed a little... well, my mom put him up to it, I could tell."

Kate laughed. "You're close with your dad, huh? More than your mom?"

"Mom and I are close, too, but Dad and I are just... buddies, you know?"

"Like me and my mom."

Joanie nodded. "Your mom is awesome."

"She is, kind of. You ready?"

"Yes." Joanie stood up, tested the rollers and then pushed forward. "Oh, man, this is weird."

Kate seemed much steadier on roller skates than ice skates and she scooted ahead, offering Joanie a hand off the carpet and onto the rink floor.

"Thanks."

"This time, you're going to have to catch me," Kate said and pushed off, quickly building up a little speed.

Joanie followed easily. The music was mostly classic rock and pop, not her taste really, but it didn't matter. The lights were bluish and pink and red and swirled around on the floor in all directions. It was a little disconcerting to look down and see the lights moving one direction when you were skating in another.

"When are you taking your driver's test?" Kate asked, slowing up a bit so they could skate and talk.

"I'm going to take it on my birthday. I'm not waiting one minute." Joanie laughed.

"When is that?"

"May fourth."

"The fourth of May," Kate repeated. "Got it."

"Oh, you don't have to do anything for my birthday."

"Oh, yes I do. I already know what it is, too."

"Kate!"

"You just hush and keep skating."

Snorting, Joanie sped up and skated away.

"Hey!" she heard Kate call behind her. "Wait up!"

They took a break after an hour or so and got some

greasy nachos and hot dogs, and they had just sat down when Zane and Samantha walked in. Kate waved them over.

"Did you invite them?" Joanie asked, thinking it was a bit of a coincidence that she and Zane hadn't been here in two years, but he just happened to show up today.

"Yes, I did. Is that okay? I thought it would be fun."

Joanie had thought about inviting them herself, but didn't know how Kate would feel about it. "Great idea," she said, patting the seat beside her as they got closer.

Zane threw his bag down in the seat. "Gonna get some food," he said, and off he went.

Samantha sat next to Kate. "I've eaten. So how are you guys?"

"Good," Kate said.

"Been out there yet?"

"Yeah. It came back really quick."

"Awesome. I can't wait."

"What size are your feet?" Kate asked Samantha.

"Eight."

"See?" Kate pointed to Joanie. "Small feet."

Joanie sighed. "Oh, fine. They're small compared to you."

Kate snorted.

"How are things with you and Zane?" Joanie asked Samantha.

"Things are good. Better than ever." Samantha smiled. "He grew up a little, you know?"

"It happens," Kate laughed.

"He never told me why you broke up, you know."

"He didn't?"

"No. I assumed it was something stupid he did since he spent like a month depressed about it." Joanie grinned.

"That figures." Zane sat down beside her with cheese fries and a hot dog.

Joanie blushed. "Sorry, Zane."

"She was jealous."

Samantha's eyes widened. "Zane!"

"She thought I was in love with you. She thought we were more than friends."

Joanie laughed out loud. "Oh, my God."

Zane sat up straighter. "Wait a minute! Oh, my God, what? I'm a good looking guy! If you liked guys you'd totally be all over me and you know it."

"Um, no," Joanie said. "For the record? No."

The whole table was laughing now and Zane pretended to pout while he ate his cheese fries.

"Don't worry, Samantha, I was jealous of Zane for the same reason at first," Kate joked.

Joanie grinned. "So there, Zane."

Kate leaned in closer. "Be nice, Joanie or I'll ask Samantha out."

"Oh, no you won't." Zane and Joanie said at the same time. Zane even glared at Kate, but Kate just laughed at him.

"Okay, you guys, I'm going skating again before Joanie hits someone."

"Shut up, Samantha!"

Zane dragged Samantha out of the booth and they went to get their skates. Joanie led Kate back out onto the rink.

"I'm never going to live that down, am I?"

"Hey, there are worse things than getting a reputation for defending yourself." Kate grinned.

"I guess."

Kate took her by the hand. "You could get a reputation

for being a lesbian."

"Oh, that would be terrible." Joanie laughed softly and gave Kate's fingers a squeeze.

Holding hands at the roller rink didn't seem to cause much of a stir at all. Sure, one or two kids looked at them strangely, but most people knew about Kate, and Joanie had already caused a scandal over Liam so maybe this just wasn't a big deal to them.

Zane and Samantha skated by them a couple of times and teased them or waved. It turned out to be a really fun afternoon.

And it only got better after they left the rink.

Kate's mother picked them up and they went back to Kate's house. Kate's room was on the third floor.

"It used to be an attic but the people who lived here before we did turned it into a room."

"It's cool up here."

"Yeah, I really like it."

The room had a bank of dormered windows along one side with dresser drawers built in where the roof started to slope. Kate's desk was on the opposite wall and that wall had a crawl space built in. Her bed was at one end, underneath a half-moon shaped window that looked kind of like an orange slice. It was covered in a fluffy, white down comforter and had four big, thick pillows plus a couple of throw pillows, one of which was covered in rainbow fabric. There was an overhead light and lots of smaller lamps around on Kate's bedside table and on her desk, and a floor lamp that sat next to a comfy looking reading chair.

Kate didn't have as much *stuff* as Joanie had. Maybe

because she just moved in and hadn't had time to really decorate her room yet? There were no posters or pictures of friends, no awards or goofy clay figurines from third grade. The room barely looked lived in, really, except for the books and notebooks and paper on the desk and the bookshelf beside it.

"Your room is so clean," Joanie said in wonder.

"Yeah, I'm kind of a neat freak." Kate shrugged. "Plus we're still unpacking boxes and there's one with some of my stuff in it somewhere – maybe in the garage. We'll get to it, I've been busy."

Joanie nodded. "So what do you do when you're not doing homework or waving a pride flag?" she teased, sitting on Kate's bed.

"Um, I watch movies, read, listen to music. I play the guitar."

"You do?"

"Badly, yeah." Kate pointed to a guitar sitting in the corner. "I'm trying to teach myself."

"I used to play the piano, but I was too lazy to practice." Joanie shook her head at herself. "I should take it up again. I liked it."

"You should."

"Do you bike at all? It's getting really nice out now and there are some great rides out in the preserve."

"I don't own a bike, but I keep thinking I should get one."

"Of course, once I get my license I may never ride again," Joanie joked.

"I'm about to start Driver's Ed."

"Oh, yeah? Ask for Gary."

"He was your instructor?"

"Yeah, he knows all about you."

"What?"

"I accidentally came out to him during my first lesson and after that he was a good sounding board."

"Oh, my God, I am so not asking for Gary."

Joanie laughed. "So when is your birthday?"

"July. I'm a Leo."

"The lion. King of the jungle. Why am I not surprised?"

"Rarrr!" Kate crawled up on the bed next to Joanie and Joanie flinched.

"Whoa, you *are* scary."

"You're pretty." Kate said softly.

"Kiss me?"

"God, I thought you'd never ask." Kate leaned forward just a little bit more and Joanie met her, their lips touching together warmly.

Joanie was still amazed at how her whole world shifted every time Kate kissed her. It wasn't about being a lesbian anymore. It wasn't about the pimple on her chin, the math test on Monday or her driver's test. The fruity scent of Kate's shampoo, her soft skin and the warmth of her lips drove everything else away and she felt full and happy. She felt safe. She felt free.

When they pulled away, Kate's smiled at her and Joanie blushed instantly.

"Stay for dinner?" Kate asked her.

"Sounds great. I'll just need to call my parents."

"Cool."

"Maybe watch a movie?"

"Only if you have popcorn." Joanie said, grinning.

CHAPTER TWENTY FIVE

May fifth was Joanie's seventeenth birthday.

"Happy Birthday!" Zane shouted as Joanie ran for the bus stop. She was panting by the time she arrived, but she beat the bus by a full minute, easy.

"Hi!" Joanie smiled. She liked her birthday. It was the one day of the year that was really hers. Her parents had always let her make her own plans on her birthday, and though she usually had dinner at home with her family, they didn't require it of her. Tonight she planned to head home for dinner with her parents and Liz, and after dinner she had a cake and coffee date with Kate.

Tomorrow morning she would take her driving test.

And her birthday started with being on time, if barely, at the bus stop. It was going to be a great day.

Zane slid into a seat on the bus and pulled Joanie in next to him. "This is for you," he said, handing her a present wrapped in bright paper that was covered in balloons. It was flat and wide and on top Zane had tied a bag of microwave popcorn and a black Pilot felt tip pen.

"For me?" Joanie practically squealed. "Thank you!" She stuffed the popcorn and the pen into her bag and then ripped open the balloon paper. "Oh, wow," Joanie pulled the journal out of the paper and held it up to admire it before opening it to flip through the pages. "I love it! The flowers embroidered into the cover are so cool."

Zane looked smug. "You're easy to buy for. You go through these things like crazy."

Joanie nodded. "One a month or so, between writing and drawing." The paper inside was soft and unlined and the leather cover smelled wonderful. "This is great. Thanks so much, Zane."

"There's an address on the first page, see it?"

Joanie looked at Zane, then flipped the book open again. "Yes. Whose address is this?"

"That's where your date with Kate is tonight."

Joanie grinned and turned slightly to look at Zane. "What are you up to?"

"Wasn't me, it was all Kate."

"Zane."

"Okay, I helped a little but it was all Kate's idea."

"She told me she had something in mind for my birthday a while ago." Joanie slid her fingers over the unfamiliar address in her new journal. She looked at Zane again. "What is it?"

"Oh, no you don't. I'm not saying a word, and I don't care what you threaten me with." Zane crossed his arms over his chest.

"Oh, come on, Zane!"

"Nope."

"Please?"

"No. No way. Kate threatened to kill me and I believe she'd do it."

Joanie sighed. "What kind of best friend are you?"

"Just trust me, it's good. And you want it to be a surprise."

"I do?"

"You do."

Joanie nodded. "Well, okay then."

But it bugged her all morning, and by lunch she was ready to force it out of Kate herself.

"If you keep this up, I'm going to cancel our date, Joanie."

"What? Kate! That's not fair."

"All's fair in love and war, isn't that how the proverb goes?"

"It's a stupid proverb. Sounds like something my mother would say, like if you keep making that face it's going to stay that way, or it's good for you, it'll put hair on your chest."

Zane nodded. "If it didn't taste bad, it wouldn't be medicine."

"Clean your plate," Samantha added, "there are children starving in Africa."

Kate snorted. "Make sure you wear clean underwear in case you get in an accident!"

"See? Stupid." Joanie stuck out her tongue.

"Well, stupid or not, you're going to have to live with it until nine o'clock. Oh, and don't bother showing up early, you won't get in."

Joanie shook her head. "What are you people up to?"

Zane looked at Kate. "Was that the bell?"

"You know what? I think it was." Kate grinned and got up from the table. Zane and Samantha were right behind her.

"Bye Joanie, happy birthday," Samantha called back.

"Pfft. See ya', losers."

Joanie looked at the bite of salad on her fork and then set it down. Now she was starting to get nervous.

It didn't help that Zane wasn't on the bus home.

Joanie went to her room to wait for dinner, took out her journal and started to draw a cartoon.

In the foreground was a big round cake with a striped candle burning in the middle. Joanie was bent over the cake about to blow the candle out and Kate, Zane and Samantha were huddled around her, laughing because this was her fourth try.

No, she thought, this was something bigger than a stupid trick candle.

A surprise party? Joanie drew a cartoon of an overstuffed couch. She drew herself, stretching out as if to take a nap. The next frame, Joanie's eyes were closed and a ton of people who'd been hiding behind it, popped up behind the couch. All you could see were eyeballs and hair, and the occasional set of fingers creeping over the back. In the last frame, Joanie was several feet above the couch, arms and legs flailing, and her eyes were enormous. The group thought bubble read, "Surprise!"

Except, if it was going to be a surprise party Kate wouldn't have made sure Joanie had the address. She'd have called from her cell phone last minute or something.

Maybe the address was a restaurant and Kate was

going to have fancy cake and coffee waiting for her. Maybe Zane and Samantha would show up with presents. Maybe it was a paint your own pottery place or a make your own jewelry shop or something. If she could have gotten onto the computer without her dad noticing she could have looked it up, but it had that stupid password on it.

An hour of brainstorming left her with tons of possibilities, and no answers. She was just going to have to wait and see. Liz knocked on her door about six o'clock.

"Hey, birthday girl, it's almost dinner time."

Joanie smiled and looked up from her journal. "Awesome. I'm starving."

"Happy birthday." Liz put a homemade card on Joanie's bed in front of her.

Joanie looked up at her little sister and smiled. "Did you make this for me?"

Liz nodded. "It's not much of a present."

"We'll see about that." Joanie opened the card. It was made out of blue cardstock and had a paper ice cream cone and the words "Happy Birthday, Joanie" done in foam letters on the front. Inside were a bunch of construction paper balloons with strings made out of yellow yarn. Each balloon said something nice about Joanie.

Joanie has pretty hair.

Joanie is very smart.

Joanie helps me with my math homework.

Joanie is an awesome sister.

And the last balloon read, *Much Love, your little sister, Liz.*

Joanie read the card over several times. Her friends talked about their little sisters like all they did was fight all the time. Sure, she and Liz had their moments, but really, they were friends. Maybe some of that was the age difference, but most of it was just that they liked each other.

"This card is a wonderful gift, Liz. Best one I've gotten so far." Joanie leaned over and gave Liz a kiss on the cheek. "Thank you."

Liz was grinning broadly. "Better than the iPod?"

Joanie nodded. "Yep. Even better."

"Wow."

"Joanie! Liz! Dinner is ready!" their mother's voice called up from downstairs.

"Coming!" they both answered at once, but Liz beat Joanie down the stairs.

Joanie's dad came in from the back porch with a plate of rare steaks and grilled asparagus. Her mom set a big bowl of garlic mashed potatoes on the table.

"This looks awesome." It smelled awesome, too. Joanie helped herself to the potatoes and then passed them to Liz.

"Joanie, I want you to know that we tried to invite Kate, but she said she couldn't make it," her dad told her.

"Yeah, I know. She and Zane have something crazy planned for tonight."

"Yes, she told us. And that got us to thinking that now that you're seventeen, we thought we'd push your curfew to eleven instead of ten."

"Yeah? Cool! Thanks." Ten was so annoying. Most movies didn't even end by ten anymore.

"And tonight, it's midnight."

Joanie looked up. "It is?"

"It's your birthday," her dad said a little too casually.

"You guys totally know what's going on don't you?"

"Would you pass the asparagus, please?"

"Dad!"

"What? I haven't had any yet." He smiled at Joanie knowingly.

"It's a conspiracy."

Her mom laughed. "It may very well be."

After the amazing dinner, Liz got up and left the room. She came back with a slightly lopsided, but delicious looking homemade angel food cake.

"Liz and I made the cake," her mother explained. It's leaning a little because it was so humid when we made it yesterday, but I think it's going to taste fine.

"It looks so good!" Joanie smiled at Liz.

It was, too. Sweet and light and just perfect. Joanie's dad was on his second helping when he brought up the driving test.

"Are you ready for tomorrow?"

Joanie nodded. "I'm a little nervous, but yeah. I'm ready."

"You're going to do fine."

"Oh, Gary called to say happy birthday and to wish you good luck."

Joanie was surprised. "Yeah? Wow, cool."

"He seemed nice."

"I figure we'll go in the morning, okay? Get it over with?"

"Sure, Dad. That sounds great."

"Good. Don't sleep too late."

Joanie snorted. "Right, okay." She stuck out her tongue, too, just for good measure.

***

Okay. So, great day, great dinner, and then onto a great date.

She hoped.

The bad thing about having no idea what she was walking into is that she had no idea what to wear. The least Kate and Zane could have done was clue her in a little on that score. She settled on a sundress that was covered in big tan and blue flowers and had a flattering empire waist. She put on flat sandals and grabbed a black sweater to go over it in case it got chilly later.

A little tszuj to her hair and she was good to go.

"Ready?" her dad asked, hearing her come down the stairs. "Hey, you look nice."

"Don't sound so shocked, Dad." Joanie rolled her eyes. "Do you need the address, or are you in on it so you know where we're going?"

"Actually, I do need the address. I know the neighborhood, but that's it."

Joanie handed over the journal that Zane had given her. "It's on the first page."

The drive was quiet, and Joanie kept a careful watch, trying to figure out where they were headed. All the streets looked familiar to her and the one in the address didn't. Eventually, after she'd accused her dad of driving in circles, he pulled into the parking lot at the YWCA.

Ten minutes late.

"My date is at the Y?"

"Yep."

"You didn't need the address at all, did you?"

"Nope. The address is fake. I think they were trying to freak you out."

Joanie snorted. "I either have the best friends in the world, or the worst," she mused, shaking her head.

"I think they're pretty damn good, if you ask me."

Joanie looked at her dad. "Yeah?"

"Yeah, I do."

"Even Kate?"

"Joanie, we like Kate; she's a nice girl. She cares about you. Anyone that cares about you is good in my book."

She hopped out of her seat and threw her arms around her dad's neck. "Thanks, Dad. I love you."

"I love you, too, Jo. Now, I'm supposed to tell you to go in through those doors there and ask for room number six."

"Six?"

Her father nodded. "Six. Go have fun."

"This is too weird." Joanie opened the car door and climbed out. "Weird. Bye, Dad."

"Happy Birthday, Jo."

She watched her dad pull out of the driveway and headed into the building. There was a girl sitting behind the counter and she smiled as Joanie walked in.

"Can I help you?"

"I'm supposed ask for room six?" Joanie answered uncertainly.

"Ah, room six. Yes."

Joanie watched her as they walked down the hall together. Was there anyone who wasn't in on this, whatever it was?

"Here you go," the girl said, opening the door for her.

Room six was small and windowless. There was a chair, a small table. On the far side of the room was a clothing rack, on which hung her prom dress. Joanie raised an eyebrow. "What's going on?"

The girl handed her a note, smiled and winked, and

left, closing the door behind her.

Smiling, Joanie sat in the chair and opened the note.

Dear Joanie, it read. *Will you please go to the prom with me? Love, Kate*

It was exactly, word for word, the same as one she'd gotten before from Kate.

Joanie swallowed hard. Her fingers began to tremble, and her heart was pounding in her chest. It wasn't often anyone got a second chance, and Joanie wasn't going to waste another second before she took advantage of it. She glanced around the room, grinning madly, and then quickly got up, pulling off her sundress and kicking off her shoes. She traded them for the skirt and the top with the spaghetti straps, an outfit that until right now she'd never wanted to see again.

Her shoes were there, too, and the little suede purse, which still had the lipstick her mother had given her in it, along with a twenty dollar bill and some tissues.

There was a knock at the door and Joanie looked up at it. "Uh, come in?"

The door opened and Kate came in. Joanie was overwhelmed, first just because it was Kate, and then because Kate looked absolutely stunning. Her dress was strapless and a dark blue, fitted on top and then the heavy fabric flowed gracefully down to her ankles. Her hair was mostly up, with a few curly strands hanging around her shoulders and more down her back.

"Kate..."

"Happy birthday, Joanie."

Joanie was breathless. "I... don't know what to say."

"Say yes."

Joanie squinted, confused. "Say...?"

Kate pointed to the note Joanie had left on the table.

"Oh!" Joanie laughed. "Oh, yes. Yes, please."

"I was hoping you'd say that," Kate said. She turned and offered Joanie her arm. "Shall we?"

Joanie blinked for a second and then shook it off, hooking her fingers around Kate's elbow.

They walked down the long hall toward the double doors at the end. Joanie heard music and gripped Kate's elbow tighter.

"What's on the other side of those doors?" she asked Kate nervously.

"Your Junior Prom," Kate replied happily. "Ready?

Joanie took a deep breath. "Sure. Yes." She nodded. "Yes, I'm ready."

Kate laughed. "Here we go." She reached out and knocked on one of the doors and as they opened, music and light spilled out of the room and washed over both of them.

"Oh, my God."

Kate laughed and tugged Joanie inside. There were a lot of people there. A lot more than Joanie would have expected. Most of them were dancing, their dresses and tuxedos bathed in bluish-purple lighting. She recognized many of them as friends from school, and others were kids she knew from other schools, too.

"Oh, my God," Joanie said again. "Kate..."

"Zane helped." Kate gestured to where Zane was standing with Samantha, both of them dressed just as they were on her first prom night.

"You guys!" Joanie rushed over to Zane and gave him a hug. "This is incredible!" She hugged Samantha, too and then ran back to Kate and took her arm again.

"I can't believe you guys did all of this for me!" Joanie's chest was tight, and she felt like she was going to cry. "I can't believe it."

"Believe it, Joanie," Kate said, then she leaned over to Joanie's ear and said, quietly, "Do you want to dance?"

Zane cut in a little while later and Kate winked at Joanie and danced away with Samantha.

"Oh, that's not good," Joanie teased as Zane watched them move away. They were talking and laughing and Zane shook his head at them.

"Shoulda known this was a bad idea."

"Thank you so much, Zane."

"Hey, any excuse for a party." He laughed. "Happy birthday."

"How did you get all these people to come?"

"I told them it was your coming out party."

"You... what?"

"And also your birthday," he added, teasing.

"Oh, God. Zane! They all know?"

"They all knew already, Joanie. You and Kate haven't made any secret of it, you know."

"Well, no, but..."

"They're here, right? What are you worried about?"

"I guess." Joanie took a good look around this time. She recognized Chris Haverford from Biology class and Tina Lawrey. James, Derek and Stephanie from math. Jenny, Allison, Bill and Kathleen from home room. And...

"Wait. Is that Liam?"

Zane followed her gaze. "Yep, that's him. And the girl with him is Amy Wilson."

"*That's* Amy Wilson?"

"Yep. You know her?"

"Well, sort of. I used to. I had a huge crush on her

once."

Zane laughed. "Did she know it?"

"Oh, God, no."

Just then, Liam looked over and caught Joanie staring. She blushed. "Uh-oh," she whispered as Liam waved to her and headed over, still holding Amy Wilson's hand.

"Hey, Joanie," Liam said a little uncertainly.

"Uh, hi?" She shifted her weight and tried again. "Liam, I'm really sorry."

Liam nodded. "It's cool, Joanie. I get why you were a little freaked out."

"A little?"

Zane laughed.

"Shut up, Zane."

"Okay, maybe more than a little," Liam conceded. "But still. It's okay."

"I can't believe you're being so nice about this. I must have seemed totally psycho."

Liam grinned. "You did. But I get it, okay? Forget about it."

"Thanks."

"Listen, you want to dance?"

"Seriously?"

"Yeah, I'm serious. You're a really good dancer."

Joanie looked at Zane.

"Hey Amy, you thirsty?" Zane asked, and whisked Amy off to get a soda.

There was no way Joanie was ever going to be able to be this good a friend to Zane. Ever.

Liam took her hand. "Let's go."

Joanie held Kate's hand and sipped her ice water.

"Kate, this has been amazing. Thank you so much."

"Thank you for going to the prom with me."

Joanie leaned into Kate. "This time."

"This is the only time that counts," Kate said, turning her head to kiss Joanie's temple.

When the music changed to something slower, Joanie set her water aside and stood, pulling Kate by the hand. "Dance with me."

Kate smiled. "Any time."

People seemed to move out of their way as they found a spot on the dance floor. Kate wrapped an arm around her waist and Joanie put her arms up around Kate's shoulders. Everything was perfect. The whole day had been just perfect. Nothing could have made it any better.

Until Kate kissed her.

A long, romantic kiss, right there in the middle of the dance floor where everyone could see. Kate's lips were soft and she held Joanie so close that it made her knees weak and her head spin. A kiss that said 'I love you' and 'happy birthday' and a million other things that words couldn't say. It was a kiss that Joanie would never forget.

Best. Birthday. Ever.

Chapter Twenty Six

Joanie sat in the front seat of her father's car, her hands in her lap, hoping the evaluator of her driving test hadn't noticed that she was wringing her fingers nervously. She thought she'd done pretty well, except for the one time she hit the brakes a little hard. And maybe she'd rolled over the stop line a little? Oh, God, she shouldn't have started to second guess herself; it was just making her more worried that she hadn't passed.

The evaluator had been totaling up points and now he was writing something at the bottom of her test. She was seriously hoping that it didn't say something like "Ms. Pierce is the worst driver on the planet."

"Okay," he said finally, then cleared his throat. He scanned over his report with his pen as he spoke. "That first stop was a little rough," he said.

"I know, I know. I don't usually do that," Joanie babbled. "I was nervous, you know? I'm sorry.

The evaluator sighed. "I know. Everyone is nervous at that first stop sign."

Joanie stop talking and held her breath.

"Your parallel parking is excellent," he said, and Joanie saw a glimmer of hope on the horizon.

Oh, please tell me I passed, she thought.

"The K-turn was nice."

"T...thank you." Joanie thought maybe she'd faint before the guy was finished talking.

"Overall a very nice job. Congratulations. Drive safe, okay?" He took off his seatbelt and opened the car door.

Joanie stared. "I passed?"

The evaluator nodded. "Yep." He handed the scored test to her dad, who was headed over to the car. "Just take that inside and give it to the ladies at the desk," he told her dad.

"Way to go, Joanie," her dad said as he got in the car. He leaned over and kissed her on the cheek.

I want to be seventeen forever. Joanie wrote in her journal that night. The words were written neatly up the side margin, right next to a cartoon of her and Kate kissing in the front seat of a car.

Joanie was behind the wheel.

She looked over at Kate, who was playing something Joanie didn't recognize on her guitar, and smiled.

Forever and ever.

I Kiss Girls